The Weight of Prejudice

Joy Michelle Austin

i

COPYRIGHT

The Weight of Prejudice

© 2025 by Joy Michelle Austin

All rights reserved.

This book was inspired by the characters of Jane Austen and reimagined in a modern setting, as well as the true story of Elisabeth Fritzl, whose strength and survival in the face of unimaginable darkness deeply influenced the themes of endurance, faith, and redemption in this novel.

Scripture quotations are taken from the ESV Bible (English Standard Version), copyright © 2001 by Crossway, a publishing ministry of Good News Publishers. Used by permission. All rights reserved.

For permissions, inquiries, or to connect with the author, e-mail:

thejoyousauthor@thejoyousliving.com

First Edition: September 2025

Printed in the United States of America

FOR MOM

When I first dared to dream,
You whispered, write.
When doubt weighed heavy,
You lifted light.

Through late-night pages,
Tears and fears,
You gave me courage
Through the years.

If ink is hope
And words are seed,
Your faith is soil—
My deepest need.

For every cheer,
Each whispered prayer,
This story blooms
Because you cared.

PRAISE FOR JANE AUSTEN'S MEN SERIES

★★ *HALF AGONY, HALF HOPE* (BOOK 1) ★★

"Half Agony, Half Hope is a gripping and heartfelt read… a compelling modern reinterpretation of Austenian heroism through a redemptive viewpoint."

K.C. Finn, Readers' Favorite

"This novel is meaty—dark yet redemptive—rich with themes of faith, healing, and redemption… At its core is a father's unshakable love, a friendship that refuses to let go, and a flicker of hope that keeps burning."

— The Literary Assistant

"One of the most emotionally gripping books I've read in a long time… Rick's journal entries add a raw, personal layer… Half Agony, Half Hope will break your heart and then stitch it back together."

Amazon Verified Purchase

"A powerful roller coaster of emotions… written with care and purpose, offering insight rather than shock. As a person of faith, I found the spiritual themes especially meaningful."

Amazon Verified Purchase

"Her prose is both elegant and evocative, painting vivid emotional landscapes...

She masterfully demonstrates how faith can transform even the most wretched

circumstances, never shying away from difficult truths yet always illuminating

pathways to healing."

Amazon Verified Purchase

★★ *But Wholly Free* (Book 2) ★★

"This devotional is a beautiful blend of raw honesty and biblical truth. Joy

Michelle Austin gently walks you through pain, grief, and guilt while pointing

you back to the hope and freedom. The connection to Rick Wentworth's story

adds a unique and heartfelt touch. If you're walking through a hard season,

this book will remind you—you are seen, loved, and never beyond God's

grace."

— The Reading Mind

"This book touched my heart in ways I didn't expect. Half Agony, Half

Hope, But Wholly Free is more than just a devotional, it's a lifeline for anyone

who's walked through pain and wondered if healing was still possible. Joy

writes with such honesty and compassion."

Amazon Review

"This devotional is raw, tender, and deeply encouraging. Joy Michelle Austin writes with grace and honesty, weaving together fiction and faith in a way that feels personal and healing. Whether you've walked through trauma yourself or are supporting someone who has, this book offers gentle hope, real comfort, and the reminder that healing is possible through God's love. A beautiful companion to Half Agony, Half Hope."

Amazon Review

WHEN THE STORM BREAKS OVER ME

When the storm breaks over me
And old agonies rise unbidden—
When I face the scorn of men,
Their pride laid bare, their hearts hidden—

Still there is a stronger voice,
Steady as the midnight star:
Christ alone, my only hope,
Near to heal each stripe and scar.

What is my comfort in this life?
Not the praise of those who stand apart—
Not the pride that guards my wounds,
Nor bitterness within my heart.

When prejudice would cast its stone,
And pride would tempt me to despair—
Still I stand on love unearned,
The cross that bears my hope and agony.

Oh, shout hallelujah—

When I am weak, still hope remains.

Oh, shout hallelujah—

Christ has borne my deepest agony.

Who steadies me when I recall

The names, the chains, the cutting word?

Who sends the waves that drive me near

To mercy's shore, where grace is heard?

Not chance nor fate nor any man—

But Christ who sees beyond the skin.

In Him no outsider is denied,

No lesser soul, no lesser kin.

If all my strength should fail again,

If anger burns or pride takes hold—

I will remember this one truth:

God alone defines my soul.

In life, in death, in everything,

No promise deeper can be said—

Christ my hope, my risen Savior,

My life, my joy, my daily bread.

Oh, shout hallelujah—

Our hope springs eternal still.

Oh, shout hallelujah—

He has carried me and mine.

And when the old year finds its close,

When breath is short and night has grown—

I will rest in this alone:

Christ will never leave my side.

We shall rise and see His face,

Where every wall at last will fall—

Until that dawn, I will proclaim:

His love is worth far more than all.

CHAPTER 1

Rick

Despite it being nine months since his rescue from captivity, Rick Wentworth still wasn't sure he deserved this—Marianne's love, Darcy's unwavering loyalty, Caroline's warmth, and the laughter of his four children filling the spaces where silence used to live.

Tonight, that laughter mingled with the scent of cinnamon and dish soap in Darcy's kitchen. The Thanksgiving feast was over, and the women had claimed the sink. Caroline Bingley, her long braids swinging, stood shoulder to shoulder with Marianne Dashwood, strategizing their Black Friday assault like generals before a siege. Caroline's Nigerian heritage and confident teacher's poise lent her a quiet elegance that Rick often admired, while Marianne's Asian-American roots shone in the dark expressive eyes Rick sometimes felt he could fall into and never climb out again.

Rick passed them a stack of pie plates, the warm air curling with cinnamon and soap. Too sweet, too safe—nothing like the sour, metallic memories that still pressed at the edges of his mind.

A small, sticky hand slid into his. He looked down at Lily, his eldest, whose grin was pure joy—unguarded, unfiltered—the kind of look that could stop him in his tracks.

"Rick," Caroline called over her shoulder, "you're coming with us, right? Outlets open before dawn."

His first instinct was to dodge. Crowds still scraped his nerves raw, noise pressing too close, too loud—a lingering reminder of the decade he'd spent locked away with his eldest child, Lily, by Louisa, the twisted psychotic woman who'd kept him a prisoner. But Lily squeezed his fingers, eyes shining.

"Daddy, can I come too? I want to see all the Christmas things."

Marianne dried her hands and smiled down at her. "What a great idea, Sweetie. It's your first Christmas here, so we need to make it extra special."

Lily's voice wobbled with feeling. "My first real Christmas ever! Will there be lights and trees?"

"Of course," Rick quickly agreed.

"And what about gifts with real wrapping paper?"

The words punched him in the throat. Memory blurred in with the present. He could clearly see Lily chained to the furnace, clutching her ragged teddy bear as though that scrap of cloth could be Christmas itself. He forced the picture back down, but guilt twisted through him like barbed wire. How could she still smile after everything she'd endured? How could she look at him as if he were enough?

Caroline's voice drew him back. "What do you want Santa to bring you?"

Lily bit her lip. "I don't know. Santa never came to the cellar where Louisa kept us. Daddy said he could be chained up too if he came to visit."

The room stilled. Rick crouched to meet her eyes. "Well, he knows where you are now, and it's safe."

She leaned into him, cheek warm against his sleeve. "It's okay, Daddy. You made me the best presents. Remember when you drew me the ocean? And you always told me such fun stories." Her voice rose with each memory, full of innocent joy.

Rick blinked against the heat pricking his eyes. He'd sketched waves on scraps of paper to keep her sane, never imagining those scribbles would become her treasures. To her it had been magic. To him, survival.

Marianne brushed Lily's bangs aside. "That picture you showed me was beautiful. But you deserve something shiny and new too, don't you think?"

Lily shrugged, hopeful. "Maybe... just one present with the fancy paper."

Rick's throat tightened. "Then that's what you'll have."

"And we need something for Ellie's third birthday," Lily added quickly. "It's her first birthday with all of us together in the real world on Saturday."

"You're absolutely right. I bet she'll want something with a duck on it," Caroline laughed, passing him a dish to dry. "So, why don't you both come shopping with us?"

He nodded. "Sure. We'll come."

Lily squealed and wrapped her arms around his waist. "Thank you, Daddy!"

Caroline grinned. "Coffee and cinnamon rolls on the way."

Despite himself, Rick laughed. "Fine. But if anyone tries to trample us for a television, I'm out."

When the night finally slipped into morning, the sky still charcoal and heavy with mist, Caroline's SUV rolled out of Croft Beach, headlights slicing through the haze. Lily sat wedged between

14

Marianne and Rick, knit hat pulled low, whispering to her stuffed lion. Darcy had given it to her at the hospital after their rescue, and now she told it all about Christmas lights and Santa lists.

Marianne handed Rick a travel mug, her fingers brushing his. The knot in his chest loosened at her touch.

"You thought any more about what you want Santa to bring?" she asked Lily.

"There's so many things. How do kids choose?"

Caroline laughed from the driver's seat. "When I was your age, I begged for a doll in Kente cloth like my mom had as a girl. Dad thought rollerblades would be cooler. Santa brought both."

"My dad bought me a telescope once because he wanted me to be an astronomer," Marianne said, smiling.

Rick cleared his throat. "All I wanted was a remote-control car. Your grandpa found one used. To me it was magic."

"Did it go fast?" Lily asked.

"Straight into walls," he said, and she giggled.

The drive passed in laughter and stories, headlights painting long streaks across the highway. By the time they reached the mall, the parking lot was already so full Caroline had to circle three times before finding a spot. Families clutched coffee cups like lifelines as they hurried toward glowing doors, the buzz of voices spilling into the predawn air. Rick tightened his grip on Lily's hand, shielding her between himself and Marianne as they threaded into the stream of shoppers.

Lily stopped just inside the toy store doors, her brown eyes wide with wonder. Lights twinkled above shelves, boxes stacked like candy-colored castles. The air smelled of plastic and peppermint from a nearby display. "It's so pretty," she whispered. "Like magic you can touch."

"Let's get some magic," Rick said.

Her eyes lit. "Really?"

"Really. If we're doing this, we're doing it right."

They walked the aisles together until she gasped at a bucket of rubber ducks—bright yellow, ridiculous, perfect. "Daddy, look! Ducks!"

Ellie loved ducks. Her stuffed duck, Quackers, had been her best friend since he and Ellie had found him at the park gift shop during their first daddy daughter outing after being reunited after the rescue.

"You're right," Rick said. "She'll love them. Since you thought of this, why don't you pick a toy too?"

"Me?"

"Yes. Because you thought of your sister first."

She hugged him so hard he almost lost his balance. For a moment, it felt like the world was whole. Safe. Maybe even redeemed.

And then—

A bright blue box of toy handcuffs caught his eye.

He saw flashes of cold tile and could see the metal biting into Lily's small ankle.

Louisa's syrupy voice: *There. Now you're where you belong.*

His chest locked. Vision tunneled. Knees wobbled.

"Rick?" Marianne's voice came soft and steady, pressing back against the noise.

"Daddy?" Lily's voice cracked.

He couldn't move. Couldn't breathe.

Marianne lowered to a crouch, switching to her no-nonsense paramedic tone. "Look at me, Rick. You're safe. You're with us. Breathe with me."

Somewhere deep inside, a verse flickered—*When I am afraid, I will trust in You.* He clung to it, shaky and desperate, matching her inhale, exhale, inhale until the fog thinned.

Slowly the room came back into focus and he could see that Caroline had Lily wrapped up in her arms, whispering gentle words he couldn't make out.

"I'm okay," he managed, voice rough.

"You don't have to be okay this second," Marianne said, fingers staying hooked around his. "Just take another breath for me."

"Why does he get scared like that?" Lily whispered, not taking her eyes off him.

Caroline smoothed a hand over Lily's hair. "Because big hurts take time to heal. But he loves you so much."

Lily's lip trembled. She nodded. "Okay."

They stayed like that for a beat—Lily in Caroline's arms, Marianne's hand steady on Rick—until his breathing evened out. As soon as he was stable and standing again, Lily rushed over and reached for him with her shaking hands.

Needing caffeine and sugar in his system after the panic attack, Rick was grateful when Caroline suggested a pick-me-up at the mall's coffee shop. After paying for their drinks they headed back into the tide of shoppers, the air thick with cinnamon rolls and sharp with perfume from kiosks. Marianne's hand brushed his as they walked, grounding him. Lily kept up easily, her knit hat bobbing like a bright beacon among the crowds.

It was as they rounded a corner that Lily slowed, her gaze caught on a store display. "Oh," she breathed.

The others followed her line of sight. In the window, beneath strings of paper snowflakes, a canvas play fort stood glowing with soft lantern lights inside. Its walls were printed with constellations and a little wooden sign hung crookedly over the flap: *Adventurer's Hideout.*

Marianne smiled, her eyes softening. "That's darling. Reminds me of when Elinor and I used to build blanket forts in the living room."

"Mine always collapsed," Caroline said wryly, though she didn't look away.

Rick lingered a beat longer, studying the fort as if Heaven had just whispered a secret to him. Something about it tugged deep inside, a picture flashed in his mind of Ellie curled up with Quackers, Lily reading by flashlight, Walter and Sam daring each other to stay inside after lights-out. A safe place. A home within a home.

"Cute," Marianne said again, tugging Lily's hand to move them along. The others drifted forward, the moment already fading into the next sale sign, the next store window.

But Rick's steps slowed. He knew, without a doubt, that he needed to get this fort for the children for Christmas. It would be the perfect gift. The thing he hadn't even known he was searching for.

He shoved his hands into his jacket pockets, catching up to the others. No one had noticed his pause, and he didn't offer an explanation. Some things you kept close until the right moment.

The tide of shoppers carried them on, but in the back of his mind the fort remained, glowing like a promise.

CHAPTER 2

Darcy

"Daddy! You're home!"

Darcy had just set out the last plate when Ellie, having heard the car pull up, burst in from the backyard, Quackers tucked under one arm.

The shoppers were quietly making their way inside. Caroline was in the lead, cheeks flushed pink, followed by Lily who was hugging a shiny gift bag like it was a treasure. Marianne and Rick trailed behind at a slower pace, arms heavy with shopping bags.

Rick set the bags down and rested a hand on Ellie's curls. "Hi, Little Love."

Ellie held up Quackers solemnly. "He came to the park with us. Uncle Darcy said it was okay."

Rick leaned heavy against the counter. "Did you say hello for me?"

Ellie nodded. "I told the ducks you were their friend too."

Sam strode in, soccer ball under his arm. "Uncle Darcy let us beat him at soccer."

"He was checking his email," Walter smirked. "That's why we won."

"I prefer to think of it as teaching you how to seize opportunity," Darcy groaned dramatically.

Marianne laughed softly as she brought in the rest of the shopping bags. "Or teaching them how to brag."

Sam puffed out his chest. "I got three goals."

Ellie tugged on Rick's hand. "Daddy, are you hungry?"

"Uncle Darcy made lunch," Walter added helpfully as he reached over to peek in the bags before having his hand playfully slapped away by Marianne.

Rick blinked like he'd only just remembered where he was. "Lunch sounds good."

"Everyone, wash up," Darcy said, giving the sandwich spread one last look. "We will eat as soon as everyone's hands are clean."

The kids scrambled toward the sink. Caroline set her purse on the counter, eyes flicking to Rick. Darcy couldn't help but see the faint shadow in Rick's smile. Even when he tried to mask it, the tremor lingered in the set of his best friend's shoulders. Darcy had seen that look before. It was the one that Rick wore when his ghosts from being held captive refused to let him be at peace.

Sensing something amiss, he touched his fiancée's hand and drew her just out of earshot into the hallway

"What happened?" Darcy asked quietly.

Caroline's eyes softened. "There was a toy handcuff set. It brought everything back for him. Marianne handled it. You'd be proud of Lily. She was so brave even though she was scared."

Darcy rubbed his jaw, the familiar frustration knotting his chest. What good was it being a billionaire if he could not pay to erase the memories that clung to his friend like chains? "I hate that he still has to fight those ghosts."

Her lips curved, bittersweet. "It doesn't go away overnight, Darcy. But he's trying. And Marianne is good for him."

"I see that," he admitted. "She's a good friend to you too."

Caroline hesitated, then lifted her gaze, voice quieter. "Do you ever think about how we started? Who I used to be?"

Darcy brushed a braid behind her ear, his tone dropping low. "More often than you think. I told Rick the day I bought your engagement ring, *'Turns out God had better plans than I did.'*"

Her breath caught.

"It's true. God's plans are better," Darcy added simply. "I thought I knew what I wanted. I thought I knew who you were, who I was, and heck, even who Lizzie was. But we all changed and thank God He brought us together. What do your romance books call it? A second chance story? That's us, darling."

Caroline's eyes glossed, and for a heartbeat he could envision the girl she used to be: ambitious, sharp-edged, and desperate to be chosen. And then he smiled because he could plainly see before him the woman she'd become: steady, warm, and the kind of woman children trusted without hesitation.

Her lips trembled into a smile. "I'm glad."

"So am I." He kissed her forehead affectionately. "If I thought you'd say yes, I'd marry you today."

She laughed, incredulous. "Today?"

"Why not? But…" His brow arched. "I suppose you'd prefer a wedding where the Stepford wives of Croft Beach have to admit they were wrong about you."

Her eyes shimmered. "Maybe I would."

"Then we'll wait," he said with a wink. "And when that day comes, they'll see what I already do."

She swallowed. "And what's that?"

"That you're the best decision I never planned."

Her answering smile wavered slightly. "I love you."

"I love you more," he whispered, and they headed back to the kitchen.

Lunch passed in warm chaos, kids talking over one another about ducks, Christmas, and sparkly wrapping paper. Ellie's laughter mixed with Sam's boasting, Walter's quick wit, and Lily's quieter wonder as she peeked into her gift bag again and again. The kitchen rang with clatter and crumbs and a kind of joy Darcy had once believed was reserved for other families. Now it lived here, in his house, spilling across his table.

"I was thinking, Rick, that since the holidays are coming up and there's a lot changing here maybe you might want to see the cottage," Darcy said, keeping his voice casual.

Rick blinked. "The cottage?"

"The beach cottage. My tenant finally moved out last week."

Sam looked up, mouth full. "You have a cottage?"

Caroline laughed softly. "Darcy has a lot of things."

Rick still looked bewildered. "I…don't understand. Why would I need to see it?"

"Because it's going to be yours. If you want it."

Lily's eyes went huge. "Ours?"

"It's a little more space," Darcy said as if they were discussing borrowing a lawn mower. "Four bedrooms, ocean view, backyard backing up right to the beach. There's a pool and a jacuzzi in the courtyard. I thought you might like the jetted tub after a long day."

Marianne made a small, choked noise and clapped a hand over her mouth.

Sam dropped his sandwich. "A pool? For real?"

Walter leaned forward, eyes wide. "Is there a barbecue?"

"Built-in," Darcy confirmed. "And a wine cooler. Though I suppose you'll be filling that with Capri Sun."

Ellie wriggled in Rick's lap. "Daddy, can we go see it now?"

Rick cleared his throat, clearly overwhelmed. "Darcy, that's—I appreciate it, but I could never pay the rent on a place like that."

"It was renting for twelve thousand a month," Caroline piped up, which didn't help Rick's expression.

Darcy nodded solemnly. "Which is why I'm offering you a special arrangement."

Rick lifted an eyebrow, suspicion creeping in. "What kind of arrangement?"

"The same rent you've been paying here," Darcy said mildly.

Rick let out something between a laugh and a cough. "Which is a measly one dollar."

"I believe the check stub says 'One dollar per month for services rendered and occasional companionship,'" Darcy deadpanned. "Consider it a standing offer."

Rick swallowed, clearly fighting emotion as Ellie babbled to Quackers about swimming in their very own pool. The sight pierced Darcy's chest. His best friend had lived in figurative cages of steel and fear for so long, and now his little girl was dreaming of swimming with her ridiculous stuffed duck. Things had changed so much in the last eight months since they had all been reunited.

When Rick looked up, his eyes were damp. "I don't know what to say."

"Say yes," Darcy suggested. "Caroline and I are getting married on New Year's Eve, she's moving in here in January, and I'd like you to have a place of your own. You need somewhere for you and the kids."

Marianne squeezed Rick's hand. "It sounds perfect."

Rick let out a shaky breath. "And maybe...maybe ours one day?"

The room seemed to all turn and look at Marianne as she blushed to the roots of her hair. "Eventually."

Caroline laughed, resting her chin on Darcy's shoulder. "This is the best thing I've heard all week."

Walter smacked Sam's arm. "We're going to live on the beach!"

Ellie threw both arms in the air. "And Quackers can swim in the jacuzzi!"

Darcy raised an eyebrow. "Let's maybe not drown the duck. Stuffed animals tend not to have good floating skills."

Rick pressed a hand to his forehead and shook his head, but he was smiling. "I don't deserve this."

Darcy gently said, "that's why it's called a gift."

The late afternoon sun slid behind the rooftops as they set off down the hill. The air smelled of eucalyptus and distant sea salt. Ellie skipped ahead, Quackers tucked proudly under her arm, trying to keep pace with the boys. Rick kept a protective hand on her shoulder, followed by Marianne and Lily who had fallen into step together, heads bent close, while Caroline's hand brushed Darcy's now and again. From here, the ocean stretched out in ribbons of silver and blue.

Even on Black Friday, Croft Beach looked more like a film set than a real place with it's brick storefronts under striped awnings, window boxes spilling with winter pansies, and shop windows glowing with holiday lights. Marianne slowed in front of Bates Books, shading her eyes to peer inside. "I've always wanted to look around in there."

"You should," Caroline said. "Miss Bates has read every book in that place. She'll talk your ear off if you let her."

Marianne smiled and fell back into step. The scent of fresh bread drifted from Priscilla Jennings' Bakery, where Caroline's gaze lingered on a tiered wedding cake in the display. "Our tasting is in a week," she murmured.

Darcy leaned closer. "Whatever you pick, I'll promise to love it."

"Even if it's fruitcake?" she teased.

"Even that," he chuckled.

They were crossing in front of the hardware store when Darcy spotted a familiar figure leaning on a lamppost, one hand resting on a polished cane. "George," he called.

The man looked up, surprise flickering across his face before smoothing into something guarded. "Darcy."

"Rick, Marianne—this is George Knightley. George, these are the Wentworths and Marianne Dashwood I've been telling you about."

George nodded politely. "Nice to meet you."

Rick shook his hand. "Good to meet you."

Marianne smiled gently. "Hello."

George's gaze flicked to the kids clustered around Ellie and her duck, something almost soft passing over his face.

"You're out early for a night owl," Darcy said.

"Needed bread." George lifted a bag, mouth twitching like he might almost smile. "And air."

"I'm showing Rick and his family the cottage. You'll be neighbors when they move in," Darcy offered.

"Nice," George said non-committal before muttering a quick goodbye as he turned, cane tapping against the sidewalk in slow rhythm.

Rick watched him go. "He okay?"

"As okay as he ever is," Darcy said quietly. "He's been through more than most."

Rick was silent a moment, thoughtful.

"You know," Darcy said lightly, "the two of you ought to start a support group. *Men Who've Survived Too Much.*"

Rick huffed a laugh. "I don't know if anyone would come."

"Probably not. But it'd be an excellent club."

Marianne laid a hand on Rick's arm. "Maybe you'll be able to get to know him better after you move in."

"Perhaps," Rick agreed.

The lane narrowed until they reached a weathered jetty stretching over the sand. Lily bolted ahead, sneakers thumping on the planks. "Daddy, you can see the whole ocean from here!" she shouted.

Rick joined her, hand on her shoulder as he took in the view of the whitecaps rolling under the lowering sun, gulls wheeling above, and houses perched along the sand.

At the jetty's end, the cottage came into view, sprawling low and wide across the sand, sun-bleached stucco and tall windows glinting in the gold light. Patio chairs were clearly visible on the other side of the low fence that bordered the courtyard.

Marianne drew a soft breath. "It looks like something out of a coastal magazine."

Rick swallowed, silent.

Caroline slipped her arm around Darcy's waist, whispering, "I knew they'd love it."

Darcy studied Rick's expression seeing the hope, disbelief, and quiet ache fight for superiority. "Ready to see inside?"

Rick didn't look away. "Yeah."

The front door opened into a wide foyer flooded with golden light. The kids darted inside, sneakers squeaking on polished tile. High ceilings arched over an open living space where welcoming couches played court to a stone fireplace.

"This is like so cool!" Sam shouted as he and Walter raced down the hall toward the bedroom.

Ellie spun in a circle, Quackers tight to her chest. "Daddy…is this all ours?"

"It's yours," Darcy said quietly. "Fully furnished. Linens, dishes, everything. There's even a bunkbed in the boys' room."

Marianne slipped her arm through Rick's. "It's beautiful."

He still hovered by the door, like stepping in might break the spell.

Ellie pressed her nose up to the sliding door leading to the backyard. "Daddy! Duckies!"

Rick finally stepped all the way in and did a pivot taking in the view.

Marianne took Ellie and Lily to see the pool while Caroline followed the boys upstairs. Darcy caught Rick's eye and tipped his head toward the master suite.

"This way."

The bedroom overlooked the ocean, sunlight pooling across the bed and armchairs at the windows. Rick crossed his arms. "This is…a lot."

"It is."

Rick rubbed his face. "I don't know, Darcy."

Darcy sat on the edge of the bed. "The commute is perfect. Five minutes to the school and church, three to my office. And…" he gestured toward the window, "…zero to your happy place."

Rick huffed something almost like a laugh. "You thought of everything."

"You'll be happy here. Or at least safe."

Rick nodded but didn't meet his eyes. "I had a bad moment in the store today. Lily was scared. Marianne and Caroline were incredible. But what if something like that happens here? What if I am alone?"

"You're going to have moments like that because you're still healing," Darcy said gently. "It'll feel too big sometimes. But it doesn't mean you're back there under her control. And if it does feel like too much? I'm just a few minutes away. Doesn't matter when it is even if it's two o'clock in the morning I want you to call me and I'll be here. No questions asked."

Rick's throat worked. "You've done enough."

Darcy shook his head. "Not possible."

Rick gave a shaky exhale. "What did Lily call you? My emotional support animal?"

"A very dignified one, mind you."

Rick almost laughed. "You ever get tired of bailing me out?"

"Never," Darcy said simply. "Besides, you're the only reason I'm interesting. Without you, I'm just a boring lawyer."

Rick finally looked over, peace flickering in tired eyes. "You're the least boring person I know."

"See? I knew there was a reason I kept you around since kindergarten."

Rick didn't argue, just stared out at the ocean, breathing like a man trying to believe he was allowed to be safe. Darcy followed his gaze. The horizon glowed with fading gold, the waves carrying a hymn older than words. For the first time all day, Rick's chest seemed to rise without strain. Darcy's own heart kept time with it, a reminder that sometimes the truest miracles were as simple as the beat of one's heart, friendship, and the relentless love of God.

Outside, Ellie's laughter drifted through the open slider, bright and sure, carrying over the soft splash of ducks in the pool. One flapped its wings, scattering sunlight in a spray of drops like tiny diamonds.

Darcy felt something in his own chest loosen. He memorized that moment—the girl safe, her father steady, the ocean breathing beyond it all—and tucked it somewhere deep. He'd keep showing up, every day if he had to, until Rick never doubted that safety was real.

CHAPTER 3

Rick

His youngest child, Ellie turned three on a Saturday morning so bright it looked like the world had been freshly scrubbed clean.

Ellie was already waiting by the front door when Rick came down the hall. Her little backpack was clutched in both hands, Quackers peeking out the top like he was king of the world.

"Daddy!" she squeaked, curls bouncing as she hopped in place. "Is it time?"

"It's time, Little Love." He crouched to zip her jacket. "Are you ready for your birthday adventure?"

She nodded so hard she nearly toppled forward. "I'm three now."

"I know." He kissed her cheek, amazed at how fast it all felt. "How did that happen so fast?"

She giggled and grabbed his hand like she thought he might forget to take her. For a fleeting second, Rick let himself think of every birthday she'd had since Louisa put her in his arms three years ago. There were cakes that had never been baked and candles never blown out. Then he shoved the ache aside. Today wasn't about loss. Today was about redemption.

The drive to San Diego was restful with Ellie softly singing to Quackers in the back, whispering her list of animals she hoped to see. Every few minutes, Rick glanced in the rearview mirror just to see her face. She was so bright, alive, nothing like the pale, hollow-eyed toddler who had clung to him in that concrete cellar on her first birthday.

That day still haunted him. He could vividly remember her tiny legs wobbling as she staggered from the cot to his lap while Lily crowned her with a paper crown. He'd hummed lullabies to drown out the creaks and footsteps above as he hoped and prayed Louisa would bring more milk downstairs.

Her second birthday had not been with them at all, a memory that still sat like a stone in his chest. Louisa had stolen her away upstairs last Thanksgiving. She had refused to relent despite his pleas and the girls' screams and tears.

"Daddy?" Ellie's voice pulled him back. "Will the penguins be awake when we get there?"

"Of course." He smiled at her reflection. "I think they're waiting just for you."

"They'll want to say happy birthday," she said seriously, like it was fact. Rick's throat tightened. She believed the world would show up for her now, and the amazing thing was that he was starting to believe it too. He whispered a prayer as he pulled into the parking lot. *Lord, let it always be so.*

The San Diego Zoo greeted them with the sharp tang of sunscreen riding on a breeze. A sea of strollers and voices swirled at the entrance gates, the kind of press of bodies that used to lock his chest tight.

He caught himself gripping Ellie's hand too hard and eased up, focusing on her joy. There was her squeal at the map shaped like a lion, her wide eyes catching the flash of a scarlet macaw overhead and the thrill of the adventure they were taking together.

When they reached the penguins, she gasped and pressed both hands to the glass. The air was cool here, the scent of chilled water strong, the rhythmic splash of wings breaking the surface.

"Hi, penguins!" she shouted.

One dove under and torpedoed past, sleek and fast, bubbles trailing like silver confetti. Ellie squealed and hugged Quackers to her chest. "Daddy, he's saying hello to us, and Quackers too. They're cousins!"

Rick couldn't help but smile. "Definitely cousins."

She turned those serious brown eyes on him. "Really?"

"Absolutely."

She squealed again and jumped in place, curls bouncing. Marveling in the moment, Rick let the sound of Ellie's joy soak through him. He almost felt lightheaded with gratitude.

They circled the zoo until his legs ached making him regret not bringing his cane, but he didn't rush her. Too many of these precious moments had been prevented by Louisa over the last three years and he wasn't cutting this one short.

In the gift shop, she went straight to the stuffed animals and picked out a small penguin, holding him close. "Quackers needs a friend," she whispered.

Rick thumbed the tag. "What's his name?"

"Flippers."

"Flippers and Quackers." He smiled. "Perfect pair."

Once their shopping adventure was complete, they ate lunch under a shady tree while monkeys swung overhead, their whoops and chatter carrying on the breeze. Ellie ate grapes one by one, studying him like she was trying to figure out something.

"Daddy, did you have birthdays when you were little?"

"I did," he said softly.

"Who made your cake?"

"Your grandma. She always tried to make it special."

Ellie reached out and patted his cheek with grape-sticky fingers. "I'm glad you're my daddy."

The words cracked something wide open inside him. For years, he'd feared he was only ever the man who failed to protect his children from the monster they knew as their mother. But here she was, beaming with youthful innocence and claiming him with joy and certainty.

"Me too, Little Love," he whispered, kissing her curls.

By the time they reached the car, she was half asleep—one arm around Flippers, the other around Quackers.

"Best birthday ever," she mumbled as he buckled her in her car seat.

She stirred again an hour later when he carried her into Darcy's house, blinking at the sudden burst of voices.

"Happy Birthday!" everyone shouted.

Her eyes went wide, mouth forming a perfect O. Balloons floated near the ceiling, streamers hung from the mantel, and a cake waited on the counter, candles lined up. Caroline and Marianne stood nearby, both grinning.

Caroline waved them over to the table. "We snuck in while you were driving back and some birthday fairies helped us get everything ready for you, Princess!"

Ellie giggled as she wiggled around until Rick set her down, then ran straight to the table. "It's for me?"

"All for you, Little Love," he said, brushing her curls back.

Lily stepped forward. "Aunt Caroline made you a cake. Three candles!"

Ellie turned serious eyes on him. "Daddy, you said Grandma made you cakes. Is she here?"

The question hit deep. "No, Sweetheart. She passed away when I was... a long time ago."

Walter frowned. "What about your dad?"

"He died when I was a little younger than Sam is now." His voice stayed steady, though his chest ached.

Lily tilted her head. "What were they like?"

Rick smiled faintly. "Your grandpa Albert worked on a farm—hardest-working man I knew. He loved sitting on the porch, telling stories with a cigar in his hand. Your grandma Rita was a cook at the hotel where Uncle Darcy and Caroline are going to get married. She made the best cannoli cake you could imagine. And she took me to church every Sunday, even when I didn't want to go." He paused, swallowing. "I haven't talked about them much because losing them hurt. But they'd have loved you kids more than anything."

Ellie slid her hand into his. "I wish I could meet them."

Rick's eyes burned. "One day, Little Love, in Heaven, you will. And until then, I'll tell you their stories so you'll always know them."

"I think they'd love you more than anything," he added softly.

"Can we light the candles now?" she asked.

Caroline handed him the lighter, and they sang as Ellie hugged her stuffed animals tight. When she blew out the candles, he could almost feel his mom's hand on his shoulder, proud and steady.

Ellie opened Lily's gift first and her eyes almost popped out at the sight of a bucket of rubber ducks. "Duckies!" She hugged Lily so hard, Quackers and Flippers tumbled to the floor.

Sam and Walter exchanged nervous glances as they handed her their gift.

"We, um, picked something too," Sam said.

Ellie peeked inside and gasped. "A swimming penguin!"

Sam grinned. "He lights up, too."

Walter rubbed the back of his neck. "We didn't know Daddy was getting you one too, but…"

Ellie hugged the penguin like he was a treasure. "I love him. You're the best brothers ever."

Sam's shoulders dropped, and Rick ruffled both boys' hair. "Perfect choice, guys."

Marianne's gift, wrapped in pale blue, revealed bath paints and sponges.

"I can make pictures!" Ellie squealed.

"They're only for use in the bathtub," Marianne warned, laughing.

Caroline and Darcy's bag held the soft duck blanket she'd found on Black Friday. Ellie rubbed it against her cheek. "It's so soft."

"Quackers and Flippers needed something cozy for naptime," Caroline teased.

"They do," Ellie said solemnly, already dragging everything toward the bathroom.

Marianne helped fill the tub while Lily lined the ducks along the edge. Ellie narrated introductions like a diplomat.

"This is Quackers—he's the boss. This is Flippers—he's new but brave."

Marianne shot Rick a grin over their heads, warm and knowing. He smiled back. The sound of their giggles echoed against the tile, a melody he never thought he'd hear again in his lifetime. Hope had once felt like a foreign language. Now it spoke fluently in bath paints and duckies.

By the time Ellie was pink-cheeked and drowsy, he wrapped her in the new blanket and carried her toward the bedroom where she and Lily slept.

"Daddy?" she mumbled.

"Yes, Little Love?"

"Can Uncle Darcy tell my story tonight? He does the voices."

Rick glanced at Darcy, who leaned in the doorway.

"You rang?" Darcy said solemnly.

Ellie nodded. "Story."

Rick kissed her curls. "If that's what you want."

Darcy settled into the chair and began weaving a story about a brave little penguin who learned to swim. Ellie was asleep before he finished.

After leaving the kids upstairs, Rick found Marianne outside on the porch swing.

"She's out like a light," Rick said.

Marianne smiled, her warm brown eyes curving into crescents with her joy. "She had the best day."

He hesitated, then brushed the pad of his thumb along her cheek. "You helped make that happen."

Her breath caught. "Rick, you're such a good father."

The words hit deep. He didn't know how to respond so he cupped her hand and asked quietly, "Do you ever think about having kids? With me?"

Her eyes widened in surprise, but quickly softened. "All the time."

Something in his chest loosened at her words, like a knot finally untied.

She stepped closer, fingers curling into his. "I should get home."

"I know." He didn't let go just yet. "Maybe just one more minute."

His lips found hers in a kiss so gentle it felt like the sealing of a sacred promise. As soon as she pulled away, brushing a finger across his lips, the loss struck as keenly as the cool night closing in around them. Rick walked her to her car, the promise of a future following them on the breeze.

CHAPTER 4

Darcy

The sanctuary hummed with the low murmur of voices and the soft rustle of coats. A faint tang of pine and beeswax wrapped the air in warmth. Advent hope breathed from the single candle already glowing in the wreath on the table beside the pulpit. The glow flickered against stained glass, splashing blue and red light across polished wood, and Darcy thought, not for the first time, that even small candles could push back a surprising amount of darkness.

Ellie clung to Rick's hand, Flippers tucked firmly under her arm like an honored guest. When Darcy had gently suggested that stuffed penguins did not need to attend church, she had given him a look usually reserved for people who kicked puppies, and he had wisely withdrawn the point.

Near the doorway, Caroline's best friend, Lucy Ferrars, stood with a clipboard hugged to her chest, hair twisted neatly, apple cheeks rosy from the cold. She gave them a small, tentative wave.

"Good morning," she said softly.

Darcy slowed, softening his voice to match her hesitance. "Morning, Lucy." She always braced for kindness like it might turn sharp without warning. He wished she knew what everyone who loved her could see. She carried a quiet strength that outshone the cruelty of Croft Beach whispers.

His good friend and their senior pastor Eddie stepped up beside her, resting one hand lightly at her back—a quiet, protective gesture Darcy had seen a hundred times. Eddie's first glance was always for his wife, and she leaned into his touch like it was the only safe place in the room before he turned to greet the rest of them.

"Morning, Darcy. Rick. Kids."

"Morning," Rick said.

Ellie proudly held up Flippers. "Hi, Pastor Eddie! This is my birthday penguin."

Eddie crouched slightly, smiling. "Well, hello, Flippers. Excellent church manners, I assume?"

Ellie nodded solemnly. "He doesn't talk much."

Lucy laughed softly, the sound shy but real, and Eddie's thumb brushed her hand in reassurance. Watching Eddie love her so openly in a town where image often outweighed kindness, always encouraged Darcy that theirs wasn't a closed-minded town. Not always, at least. There were cracks of light. And sometimes, they came in unexpected friendships and unlikely marriages.

Lucy cleared her throat. "I saved you guys seats near us if you like. I can tell Caroline when she shows up."

"Thank you," Darcy said, meaning it.

"And after service, there's a meeting about the Nativity play, if anyone's interested…"

Ellie gasped so hard she nearly tipped over. "I want to be an angel, Daddy! With sparkle wings!"

Rick sighed, already resigned. "All right, Little Love. We'll see about sparkle wings."

Sam looked at Darcy, hopeful. "You'll stay too, right?"

Darcy inclined his head. "Yes, I'll stay. Someone has to keep you from staging a coup over casting."

Pastor Eddie grinned at Rick as they watched the kids hurry off to Sunday School before turning to Darcy. "You're still good for dinner tonight? Lucy has something in the crock pot that smells amazing."

The service ended with the final notes of the hymn still echoing through stained glass. Families lingered in small knots of conversation while children zigzagged between pews, their voices bright against the hush. The air carried that peculiar mixture of coffee from the fellowship hall and hymnals that had been handled by a hundred hands. It was the smell of ordinary things that together became sacred.

Lucy stood near the piano, clipboard clutched tight enough to whiten her knuckles. A line of children shuffled forward, whispering and fidgeting, parents hovering nearby, pretending they weren't watching.

This was Lucy's first year directing the Nativity play since Ned and Fanny had retired meaning Fanny was no long the children's ministry pastor. Judging by Lucy's expression, she already regretted saying yes to helping with the play.

Caroline spotted a young Hispanic girl standing off to one side, twisting the hem of her blue dress. "Maria!" she called gently, waving her over.

Maria's eyes lit with relief as she hurried to Caroline's side.

"This is Lily," Caroline said warmly, with the gentle affection she gave all her students. "You girls are about the same age."

Maria smiled shyly. "Do you want to be Mary too?" she whispered to Lily.

"Nah." Lily grinned. "I want to be an innkeeper."

Darcy felt warmth stir in his chest. Caroline had a way of pulling people in without fanfare, giving kindness freely in a town where it wasn't always safe to do so. It was one of the reasons he loved her. There was no doubt that she lived her faith out loud, no spotlight required.

As soon as sign-ups officially began, Ellie was practically vibrating as she bounced forward to join the crowd of young angel choir hopefuls. "I want to be an angel! Because I already have wings. And I sparkle!"

Rick muttered, "We're still finding glitter from yesterday's birthday party."

Lucy smiled, her voice steadying. "Perfect choice, Ellie." She made a note.

Lily stepped forward. "I want to be the innkeeper. The nice one who lets them use the manger."

"That's wonderful," Lucy said, visibly relaxing. She probably had assumed all the girls had wanted to have their chance at Mary but Darcy knew that Liliy would always be that unique and different one no one could predict.

Sam and Walter followed with matching grins. "Wise men," Sam declared.

"Yeah, wise men," Walter echoed, elbowing his brother.

Darcy nudged Rick. "Remember when we were wise men in sixth grade? You tripped and took us out like bowling pins."

Rick huffed out a laugh. "Some things never change."

When Lucy called finally for girls who want to play Mary, a good-sized cluster of girls stepped forward including Ava Collins, the only child of William Collins, the community pastor, and his wife, who insisted on being called Mrs. Collins despite only being in her mid-thirties. After a beat, a hesitant Maria also stepped forward. One by one the young girls read a Scripture verse. Finally it was Maria's turn and clutching the Bible like a lifeline, she took a deep breath and read, voice trembling but clear: "And she gave birth to her firstborn son and wrapped him in swaddling cloths and laid him in a manger, because there was no place for them in the inn."

Darcy swallowed hard. The verse he had heard since childhood landed different coming from Maria. Her voice was fragile, trembling, and yet steady with courage. Wasn't that the Gospel in miniature? God choosing the overlooked, the quiet, the underestimated.

Then a voice sliced through the room.

"Excuse me."

Mrs. Collins stood near the doorway, arms folded, wearing the polite but razor-edged smile she used like a weapon.

Maria froze, knuckles whitening on her card.

Lucy startled. "Oh—hello, Mrs. Collins."

"I was wondering," Mrs. Collins said sweetly, "why my sweet Ava wasn't immediately considered for Mary. People expect the Holy

Family to look… a certain way. The baby Jesus is white. Mary should be too."

The words hit Darcy like ice water. His jaw locked, hot anger surging in his gut. How could she? It was not just a below the belt cruel remark about Maria but also signified how much prejudice was still Croft Beach's native language. Across the room, Caroline's young Hispanic student's chin trembled as she stared down at her shoes, small and silent under the weight of prejudice.

Lucy's clipboard shook slightly. "I thought it would be fair to let everyone read."

Caroline stepped forward, her voice calm but edged with steel. "Maria has worked very hard. She deserved the chance to try out, just as much as your Ava."

Mrs. Collins's smile thinned. "My husband is the community pastor. It will look odd if our daughter isn't Mary."

Lucy's voice strengthened, likely surprising even herself. "Maria read beautifully."

"And she deserves the part," Caroline added, resting a warm hand on Maria's shoulder.

For a long moment, no one moved. Darcy felt the whole room holding its breath.

Then Lucy squared her shoulders. "Maria will be our Mary."

Maria gasped, covering her mouth, tears shining in her eyes.

Mrs. Collins stiffened, clearly ready to argue, but Eddie's calm voice carried from behind them. "Looks exactly right to me."

The room went still. Even the whispering children quieted.

Maria lifted her head, shoulders squared, and whispered, "Thank you."

Ellie tugged Rick's sleeve, oblivious to the tension. "Daddy, can we get angel wings now? The sparkly kind?"

Rick exhaled, glancing at Darcy. "Some things never change."

Darcy looked at Maria, standing tall now thanks to Lucy and Caroline's support, and shook his head slightly. "No," he said quietly. "Some things do, you know. We serve an awesome God."

Later that evening after dinner had been cleared up, Caroline reached across the table and squeezed her best friend's hand. "When do you want to go shopping for your matron of honor dress?"

Lucy blinked, startled. "You… you still want me to stand up there with you?"

Caroline frowned softly. "Of course I do."

Lucy's eyes lowered. "Caroline, you're… so beautiful. Everyone says you look like an exotic model. And I'm… just me. Maybe Marianne would look better next to you. I could still help… just in the background."

Caroline's voice softened but carried an edge of steel. "I don't want you in the background. You've been my best friend in Croft Beach since I became a Christian. You stood by me when no one else did. That means more than what Croft Beach thinks we should look like."

Lucy's lip trembled. "You really want me?"

Caroline leaned forward, taking her hand. "I really want you. Just as you are. In fact, if you go on a diet, I'll be very mad at you."

Eddie squeezed Lucy's other hand, eyes warm. "And if you're worried about standing next to a model…" He glanced at Darcy, mouth twitching. "You forget she's marrying a man with questionable taste in hair styles."

Darcy snorted. "Harsh, Eddie. And that coming from a man who once thought frosted tips were a good idea."

Caroline swatted Eddie's shoulder, laughing. Lucy sniffed, but there was a hint of a smile now, and a quiet nod. "Okay. I'll try."

Darcy sat back, watching Caroline's hand wrapped around Lucy's, Eddie's hand covering hers as well. In that small triangle of love and loyalty, he saw what he hoped Croft Beach might one day become. It was a place where kindness outweighed appearances, and faith spoke louder than prejudice.

CHAPTER 5

Rick

The weather was stubbornly warm for December, the sky bright as polished glass as Rick carried the last of the boxes into the cottage. The sunlight off the ocean threw gold across the stucco walls, and for a second Rick had to pause on the threshold, almost dizzy with gratitude. A year ago, the only walls around him had been concrete, the only air damp and metallic. Now, this warmth, light and laughter were his. A gift he still wasn't sure he deserved.

There was not much to carry. Darcy had already furnished everything, right down to brand new towels and matching dishes. But everyone insisted on helping anyway, crowding the living room with takeout bags, extra blankets, and the kind of good intentions that made the place feel more like home than any furniture catalog ever could.

Ellie darted from room to room, Quackers under one arm and Flippers under the other, announcing plans as she went. "Daddy! Where will the Christmas tree go?"

Rick set down a box of books and crouched. "Where do you think it should go, Little Love?"

She tapped her lip, squinting like a miniature architect. "By the window. So the angels can see it."

"Good idea," Lily agreed, slipping past with an armful of pillows and blankets for the den. Maria followed shyly, carrying the board games and puzzles the kids had found at HomeGoods.

Maria's mom, Graciela, who taught alongside Caroline at Jane Austen Academy, stood in the kitchen with Marianne and Lucy, unpacking the last of the dishes. She glanced up and smiled. "Ready to kick us all out of your house yet, Rick?"

"Never," he replied honestly. It was nine months since their rescue from the basement where Louisa had kept him and Lily and yet he still found it hard to fathom he and the children had a home of their own. His throat tightened as he glanced at his daughters. Ellie was skipping along as Lily hummed to the tune on the radio as she went about her work arranging her favorite games in the den cupboard. *This is what freedom sounds and looks like.*

The front door opened, and Marianne's elder sister, Elinor, breezed in, breathless from her run to pick up salads and pizzas. She'd been staying with Marianne for the past few days, between jobs. Her presence was composed and self-assured as ever, her opinions landing with precision that could fill a room faster than pepperoni filled the air.

When Marianne first mentioned she had two sisters, Rick's private fear was that one of them might be a twin—another Louisa or Anne in disguise. He had definitely had his share of twins. Thankfully, while Marianne and Elinor shared raven-black hair and brown eyes that nearly disappeared when they smiled, the similarities stopped there. Marianne was gregarious and open; Elinor, reserved and calculating. Marianne was curvy and petite, with a dusting of freckles across the bridge of her nose that Rick found irresistibly kissable; Elinor's skin was porcelain-smooth, her model's frame all endless legs and striking proportions.

Eddie relieved Elinor of the food with an easy smile, brushing her hand in thanks. It was nothing, really—a friendly touch—but it did not go unnoticed. Lucy's hands, in fact, stilled on the dish towel, eyes dropping for a beat before she resumed stacking plates. Marianne's gaze flicked between Elinor and Eddie and then to Rick, silent but aware before she crossed to the couch and sat beside him, her smile warm but quieter than before. "Does it feel real yet?"

Rick looked around his living room. Elinor was setting up the pizzas on the kitchen count with Graciela's help. Eddie and Lucy stood in the corner deep in conversation. Caroline sat curled on the sofa with a wedding binder she never went without, Darcy's arm draped across the back as he murmured something that made her laugh. His new neighbor, George, had been wrangled into helping out and now stood near the window, hands in his pockets, watching the boys swimming in the pool with a sadness that Rick could feel from across the room. The weight of grief clung to George like a second skin, and Rick's chest tightened at the sight because he knew that weight, knew how it dragged at your ribs until even joy felt dangerous.

"Almost," he finally admitted as he returned his attention to the woman he loved.

Marianne slid her hand into his, fingers warm and steady. "It will," she promised.

Ellie's voice cut through, joyful and pure: "Daddy, can we put the angel on the tree together?"

"Of course, Little Love. But how about some pizza and salads first?"

They ate lunch around open boxes, laughing when Walter declared one slice of pizza "the best food ever" simply because it was eaten cross-legged on the floor instead of at a table. Graciela coaxed Maria to eat a carrot stick while Ellie tried to share her pizza with Flippers and Quackers, neither of whom seemed impressed. The boys argued about which superhero would be best at hanging lights, while Lily announced her future bakery would serve

"Christmas pizza" every December, extra cheese included. Rick leaned back against the wall, heart swelling at the ordinariness of it all. Ordinary was everything he'd prayed for.

Everything was practically perfect until Rick heard Marianne's voice drift in from the hall. "Elinor, I know Eddie is a friendly guy, but... be careful."

Elinor's reply was light, almost amused. "Careful?"

"His wife is sensitive. Lucy doesn't have your confidence."

A pause, then Elinor's shrug was almost audible. "We're just chatting about college memories Is that a crime?"

Marianne returned to the living room, a faint crease between her brows, not saying more. The way she wrapped her hands around the coffee cup Rick handed her told him something was brewing.

After lunch the moving party started to break up with Darcy and Caroline leaving on a wedding mission and Graciela and Maria headed out to a birthday party. As Lucy and Eddie were saying their farewells to Marianne, Rick crossed over to where George stood poised to silently leave by the sliding back door. "We're heading out soon to pick a Christmas tree. Want to come?"

As everyone departed for their own afternoon plans, George hesitated. Something like longing flickered in his eyes before he looked away. "Haven't had a tree in a long time. Not since..." His voice trailed off. "Not since Emma. And the baby."

Darcy had already told Rick it had been eight years since that car accident—eight years since George lost his wife and the unborn son they'd been expecting. Rick couldn't imagine eight years let alone eight hours in that cellar without his kids; those years without them would have broken him undoubtedly.

"If you want to join us in hunting down the perfect Christmas tree, you're welcome," Rick said gently.

Walter, who'd been headed toward the garage with the empty pizza boxes, looked up, eyes wide. "You had a baby?"

George blinked, startled. "We… were going to. A little boy. He would have been about your age, I reckon."

Walter nodded solemnly. "I'm eight."

A rough sound escaped George—half laugh, half sigh. "That's a good age."

Walter squared his shoulders. "I'm going to call you Uncle George. That way you have family again."

George blinked fast, then looked away. "Thank you," he whispered.

Walter glanced at Rick. "Is that okay, Dad?"

Rick rested a hand on his son's shoulder. "That's more than okay."

George's throat worked, eyes glassy. "I think… I'll come with you. If that's all right."

"That's perfect," Rick said, warmth settling deep in his chest.

Across the room, Ellie squealed, "tree time!"

The tree lot was crowded, strings of lights swaying overhead and the sharp, sweet scent of pine heavy in the air. The kids scattered like a pack of elves, each determined to find the *perfect* tree. Laughter spilled around them, mixed with Christmas music blaring faintly from a tinny speaker near the entrance. Rick's hand twitched with old instinct to shield his children from the crowd, but then Marianne slipped her arm through his and whispered, "We're safe," and he believed her.

Ellie clutched Rick's hand, pointing with her free one. "That one!"

"It's taller than the roof," he said, biting back a laugh.

"But it's beautiful," she insisted, then spotted a scrap of gold tinsel clinging to the stand and gasped. "Daddy, glitter! Look! It's magic!"

Rick chuckled. "Everything with glitter is magic, huh, Little Love?"

Walter and George drifted toward a corner with six-foot trees. Walter gestured earnestly with both hands, and George bent slightly to listen, nodding like every word mattered. For the first time, George's shoulders weren't so tight. Rick caught a glimpse of the man George might have been before grief hollowed him out.

Marianne stepped up beside Rick, hands tucked into her jacket pockets. "They look like they've been friends forever," she said softly.

"Walter's appointed himself George's guardian angel," Rick murmured. "He might be right for the job."

Her smile softened, then hesitated. "So what do you think of my sister?"

He shrugged. "She seems… a little intense. I don't think I'm her favorite person."

Marianne bit her lip. "Elinor is… well, Elinor. She has opinions about everything. Strong ones."

Lily's triumphant cry broke before either of them could say more. "Daddy! I found it!"

She stood beside a tree only slightly taller than she was, hands on her hips like she'd conquered Everest.

Walter gave George a thumbs up. "Uncle George says it's a good one."

"Then it's the one," Rick said.

They tied the tree to the roof of Rick's SUV. Ellie pranced beside Rick, singing an off-key version of *Away in the Manger* as he and George secured the ropes. Her little voice carried into the air, thin but sure, and Rick thought maybe Heaven leaned close to listen.

When everyone piled back into the cars, George climbed into the seat beside Walter, listening to him chatter about the merits of top bunks and Christmas lights. Rick shot up a prayer that Walter could help George heal.

Back at the cottage, they set the tree by the window just like Ellie planned. The kids swirled around it with lights and ribbons, Ellie crowning Quackers and Flippers as "tree guardians."

Rick stood still for a moment, soaking it in. The sparkle of Christmas lights caught the joy in the room. Walter explained to George the importance of even ornament spacing, Lily handing Marianne a star to hang, and Sam and Elinor looping a strand of red beads around the branches. Then Ellie ran up to him, pressing her cheek against his leg and whispering, "It's perfect, Daddy."

He scooped Ellie up, drawing her close to his heart, her warmth sinking into him. "Yeah," he said softly. "It really is."

George looked over from the tree, Walter perched on his hip like it was the most natural thing in the world. The man's eyes were still damp but softer now, his shoulders finally easy.

Rick sighed. This house wasn't just full of boxes and borrowed furniture. It was full of family. And that felt like a kind of miracle all its own. A miracle wrapped not in grandeur, but in pizza boxes, pine needles, and the sound of children laughing, and maybe that was the truest kind of miracle there was.

CHAPTER 6

Darcy

Darcy had always assumed wedding planning would be tedious with endless meetings, too many opinions, and far too much money spent on details no one would remember.

He hadn't accounted for the way his beautiful fiancée's face lit up when she talked about colors or playlists. There was the adorable way she tucked a braid behind her ear when she was nervous about a choice and the way she gripped her lucky pen like a weapon whenever someone second-guessed her. Seeing everything through her eyes made him enjoy every minute of the experience. That was until they sat down for their taste testing at Priscilla Jennings' bakery on Main Street and everything came to a screeching halt.

The bakery smelled of sugar and vanilla with Priscilla's signature pastries and cakes glittering under glass. Priscilla Jennings, whom Darcy had known since his childhood, greeted him warmly. Her professional smile faltered slightly however when Caroline mentioned her idea.

"I was thinking we could have one layer of fruit cake," Caroline said, referencing her notebook where she had photos of her parents' wedding cake. "My parents had fruit cake and coconut at their wedding. I know we can't do coconut because of Darcy's allergy, but the fruit cake would feel like they are there with us."

Priscilla hesitated, just long enough to register doubt. "Fruit cake is rather heavy and a bit old-fashioned."

Caroline's shoulders stiffened, just enough for Darcy to feel the shift. He knew that she had her ideas dismissed like this too many times before, whether it was in staff meetings, or pews, or at coffee counters where women with polite smiles let their prejudice show in sharper ways. Every time it happened in front of him, he was hit by the same helplessness, desperate to protect her but lost for how, and it drove him crazy.

"I know," Caroline finally said. "But I'd like it anyway."

The baker glanced Darcy's way as if looking for his support. "Most couples choose vanilla or lemon. Some will choose red velvet if they're feeling daring. But fruit cake is definitely not what couples of Croft Beach are going for anymore."

Darcy put his arm around Caroline's shoulders as he looked at the other woman. "Caroline and I could care less about what other couples are having at their weddings."

Priscilla blinked at his tone.

"If she wants fruit cake, she gets fruit cake." What he wanted to say but wasn't sure how to put in words was that he would spend his whole life fighting off smallness like this for her if only to prevent the light in her eyes from disappearing. In fact, he'd be willing to pay Priscilla Jennings off and buy the bakery himself if it came down to it.

Silence pulsed in the small space.

Taking the initiative, Caroline cleared her throat and turned to look at Darcy with a smile on her face and gratitude in every syllable. "No coconut, though. I'd rather keep you out of the hospital on our wedding night."

For one irrational second, Darcy wanted to say *add it anyway*, just to prove Caroline didn't have to keep giving things up to please everyone in this ridiculously small-minded town. Instead, he said, "Actually, put it in as a separate layer."

Caroline's head snapped toward him. "Darcy—"

"I mean it. This is your wedding. You deserve whatever your heart wants. That includes coconut, even if it makes me break out in hives for our honeymoon."

She chuckled and leaned forward to kiss him as if she wanted him to feel just how grateful she was.

Priscilla Jennings gave a brisk nod when the kiss ended and anxiously picked up her own notebook. "One fruit cake layer, one coconut layer and the last layer we will keep traditional? Vanilla perhaps?"

Caroline nodded. "Yes. Thank you."

Priscilla nodded as she rushed away to get the frosting samples and Darcy looked long and hard with admiration at Caroline. She'd been doing this all her life, he realized. Standing tall in the face of smallness.

When they finally stepped outside, the air had turned brisk. Caroline tucked the order sheet into her bag and pulled her coat tight.

"Come on," Darcy said quietly, tipping his head toward the dunes across the street. "Let's go take a walk."

She nodded, falling into step beside him. The wind swept her braids into the air, wild and lovely. Her brown fingers lacing tightly with his paler ones.

They said nothing for a while. The beach was mostly empty, save for a few gulls overhead and the steady pulse of waves. Yesterday had been loud when they helped Rick and the kids move into the

60

beach house. It had been full of laughter echoing off tile floors and the adorable Ellie narrating duck introductions like a tour guide. Today was supposed to have been joyful too. Instead, it had scraped up something hurtful that had left a bitter taste in Darcy's mouth.

Unable to take the silence, Darcy drew her close, savoring the perfect fit of her in his arms.

"Who needs dessert anyway when they have us—chocolate and vanilla, the swirl no one saw coming."

Pulling back from his embrace, Caroline arched a brow looking up at him as if she was trying hard not to laugh. "Did you just compare us to ice cream?"

"Why not?" Darcy laughed, leaning in closer. "You're the rich, decadent scoop everyone craves and I'm your vanilla—simple, steady, and hopelessly hooked on you."

After kissing her until he needed air, Darcy smiled. "What would your parents say if they were here?"

She hesitated. "About us?"

"About the wedding."

Her thumb brushed his knuckle. "My mom would fuss over everything such as the flowers, songs, and insist I wear something blue. She'd probably bake her own coconut cake just to ensure it is perfect."

Darcy smiled, picturing an older version of Caroline with a sparkle in her eyes as she worked tirelessly in the kitchen making sure everything was perfect.

"And your dad?"

Her voice dropped. "He always told me the same thing, whenever someone made me feel less."

Darcy waited.

"'Some folks are so small inside they can't see past their own reflection. You just keep standing tall, Princess. You're exactly who God meant you to be.'"

Darcy's throat tightened. He could almost see her, a little girl with braids and bright eyes, holding onto her father's words like armor.

"He was right," he murmured, bending to kiss her palm for a brief second.

She looked at him then, eyes luminous in the dimming light. "He'd probably pull you aside and tell you loving me means you'll face that smallness too, but that it doesn't change who we are."

"It doesn't." His voice was hoarse. "It never will."

Her smile wobbled. "I know."

"For the record," he added gently, "if your mom had insisted on coconut cake, I'd have eaten around it just to make her happy."

Caroline gave a wet laugh. "And I'd have hidden the EpiPen in the pocket of my wedding dress."

He stopped walking and turned toward her, cupping her cheek in his hand. "You belong," he whispered. "With me. In this town. Everywhere."

She didn't flinch from the words. Her breath caught, but she didn't look away. "And you belong with me," she said softly.

The tide surged closer, cold foam brushing against their shoes. He kissed her slow and steady, his hand cupping her cheek as though she were the rarest treasure. For one fleeting moment, he wished her parents could see them. If only they could see her now, perhaps they would be at peace knowing she was cherished for exactly who she was.

When it came down to it, the town didn't matter. What mattered was their love and moments like this with the salt air in their lungs and Caroline's hand warm in his. He could take comfort in knowing the unshakable truth that together, they could weather anything.

CHAPTER 7

Rick

Pastor Eddie's office wasn't big—barely bigger than the cellar that still haunted his dreams sometimes—but it never felt cramped. Maybe it was the soft light spilling through blinds or the gently repurposed leather couch with a hand-quilted throw folded across the back.

He'd spent too many hours on that couch earlier this year, when even walking into a sanctuary felt like his lungs were caving in. When Darcy first brought him back to Croft Beach after a month in the hospital, he'd been a man held together with duct tape and sheer stubbornness determined to make things work out for his children's sake.

Seeing Rick at the door, Eddie took off his glasses and smiled that easy, patient smile that always made it feel safe to talk. "Hey, Rick. Come on in."

Rick dropped onto the couch, stretching his legs. "Hope I'm not interrupting."

"You're saving me from budget spreadsheets," Eddie said dryly. "Believe me, you're doing me a favor."

Rick huffed out a laugh and leaned back, feeling his shoulders unclench a little.

Eddie studied him—not in a way that pried, but the way he always did, like he actually cared what lived behind your answers. "How are you?"

"Better," Rick admitted. "Not perfect, but better."

64

"The panic attack still sticking with you?"

Rick rubbed his palms on his jeans, heat rising in his chest at the memory. "Yeah. It came out of nowhere. One minute I was fine, the next..." He swallowed. "I was back there."

"You reaching out? That's progress," Eddie said quietly. "You're not hiding anymore."

Rick's throat tightened. "Still feels like we don't really belong here sometimes."

"You're not the only one who feels that way. Lucy does. Caroline. Even Marianne, in her own way. This town likes tidy boxes."

"And we don't fit."

"No," Eddie said simply. "But that's why God uses people like you."

Rick let out a shaky breath, thinking of Lucy standing her ground at the Nativity auditions, her voice steady despite the tremble in her hands. "Your wife was brave."

"She's terrified she'll lose her place as the new Children's Ministry leader if she makes a wrong move," Eddie said softly. "I could not be prouder of her, though."

"She was braver than half the parents in that room," Rick muttered.

"And look at you, Rick. You stayed here in Croft Beach," Eddie pointed out. "You didn't run."

Rick shook his head. "It doesn't feel brave. Where else would we go?"

"It never feels brave." Eddie smiled quietly. "That's how you know it is."

Rick's gaze drifted to the framed verse behind Eddie's desk: *For He Himself is our peace.*

"This week's sermon is on peace," Eddie said, following his gaze. "Not just the absence of conflict. *Shalom. Eirēnē.* Wholeness. Being made complete again, even when things are messy."

Rick stared at his hands. "Does that mean I can have peace even when I still feel broken?"

"It means you can have peace because you know Who holds you together. You're doing better than you think," Eddie said quietly.

When Rick finally stood, Eddie came around the desk, resting a hand on his shoulder. "You're not alone, Rick."

Outside, the winter sun was already tilting gold. Rick drew in the salt air, letting it clear his head as he walked toward Jane Austen Academy.

The kids spilled out of the doors as he walked up, their voices high and bright. Caroline crouched near the steps, one hand on Maria's shoulder, speaking low and gentle. Maria's backpack strap twisted in her fingers. Rick recognized the way she looked everywhere but up.

Lily bounded toward him. "Daddy, can Maria come over? She can help me with math."

Caroline smiled faintly. "Her mom and I have a faculty meeting."

Maria peeked at him, hesitant.

"You want to call her, make sure?" He handed over his phone.

"Hi, Mami... Mr. Wentworth said I could go to Lily's house... Is that okay?" Maria whispered. After a pause, her mouth curved. "Okay. *Muchas gracias.*"

She gave the phone back, ducking her head.

"She said yes?" Rick asked.

Maria nodded.

"Perfect. Ellie's at Chloe's house, so it's just you, Lily, Sam, and Walter."

Walter grinned. "Cool."

Caroline squeezed Maria's shoulder before standing. "I'll walk your mom to Rick's house later."

"Thanks," Rick said.

Her eyes softened. "Anytime."

Lily nudged Maria as they walked up the path to the beach cottage. "Doesn't the house look really pretty?"

Maria whispered, "It's really nice."

Walter, stepping out of his sneakers, called over his shoulder, "Our old house was bigger."

The room went still. Sam looked down. Lily's jaw clenched.

Walter plowed on, oblivious. "We had this giant pool, and Mommy let us have a floating dinosaur."

Lily spun on him, words sharp and shaking. "Yeah, well, Dad and I wouldn't know, would we? Since we were chained in a cellar."

Maria's eyes went huge.

Walter froze, blinking hard.

"Lily," Rick said quietly.

Her shoulders were tense, her face set, but she turned away, guiding Maria to the kitchen with quick, stiff movements.

Walter's voice broke the silence. "She wasn't always bad."

Rick's chest ached. "I know."

"She's still my mom," Walter whispered.

"I know that too."

From the kitchen, he caught sight of Lily, stiff as a soldier forcing herself upright, reaching for one of the homemade blueberry muffins she'd baked yesterday. She was whispering something he couldn't hear to Maria. He wanted to talk to his eldest, but his son needed him more, so he stepped through the sliding door.

As expected, he found Walter curled up by the pool, knees tucked to his chest, staring blankly ahead. Rick dropped onto the step beside him.

"I didn't mean to make her mad," Walter said.

"I know, Buddy."

"She wasn't always mean. Sometimes she let us eat popcorn in the living room or stay up late."

"That sounds nice," Rick said gently.

"Is it bad I miss her?"

"No." His throat tightened. "It's not bad."

"But Lily says she's a monster."

Rick exhaled. "Sometimes people are two things at once. They can hurt us and still be someone we love."

Walter hesitated. "Do you miss her?"

He thought of the woman who'd used him like a sperm ATM, given birth to his children, and kept him chained in that disgusting cellar for a decade. "No," Rick said quietly. "But I'll always be grateful that she gave me you and your brother and sisters."

Walter's voice wavered. "Do you think she ever loved us?"

"I think she loved you the only way she knew how."

Walter's eyes flicked up. "Do we have to hate her?"

"No. You just have to be honest about what's in here." Rick tapped his chest.

Walter nodded hesitantly. "Can we... see her for Christmas? Just me and you. I don't want her to think that I forgot about her."

The ache sharpened, but Rick nodded. "Yeah, Buddy. If that's what you want to do."

Walter leaned briefly against him before wiping his eyes. "Snacks now?"

Rick smiled faintly. "Yeah. Snacks."

After homework was complete, Maria had relaxed enough to play a board game with Lily while Walter and Sam worked on setting up their bedroom. By the time Graciela picked Maria up, she hugged Lily goodbye naturally, like she'd been coming to the house for months.

Afterward, the kids curled up on the couch, too wrung out from all the feelings to move. Rick ordered a pizza and started a Christmas movie on the flatscreen before he stepped outside where the porch swing beckoned to him.

Warm fingers caressed his cheek, and then Marianne's lips, soft, sure, and full of promise, brushed his.

"Hi," she whispered.

"Hi, gorgeous."

She slid onto the swing, tucking herself under his arm like it was the most natural thing in the world. "How was today?"

"Complicated."

He told her everything—Walter's memories, Lily's anger, Walter's wish to see his mom.

"You said yes?" she asked gently.

"Yeah."

"You did a good job, Rick."

"I don't know about that."

"It was," she said softly. "You didn't promise him it'd be easy. Like a loving father, you showed Walter and all the children that they wouldn't be alone."

He stared out at the yard, listening to the soft hush of waves beyond the fence. "Feels like I'm messing it up."

Her palm settled over his heart, warm and grounding. "You're not. You're showing them that love doesn't end when people disappoint us. That it's okay to hope, even when it hurts."

Something in him broke loose, his chest tight with gratitude and exhaustion. She reached into her coat pocket, thumb moving over her phone. A moment later, the delicate strains of Prokofiev's *Romeo and Juliet* floated from the phone's speaker. Of course, it was the music he always turned to when his mind wouldn't settle.

He turned to look at her, impressed. "You remembered."

Her smile was quiet, almost shy. "You said once it helps you breathe."

It did. God, it did.

He kissed her slow, steady, and with everything he hadn't been able to say, and when she finally pulled back, she whispered, "I love you."

CHAPTER 8

Darcy

Darcy had booked the Holiday Lights Cruise weeks ago because he knew Caroline would call it extravagant and then smile all night like a kid at Disneyland. The thought of her musical laughter under strings of lights, head tipped back with wonder, had carried him through more than one long day in court.

Darcy's beloved housekeeper Mrs. Reynolds had agreed to watch the kids. When Darcy had asked if she was sure about all five— Rick's four plus Maria—she'd given him that look perfected by thirty years of wrangling Darcys.

"Go," she'd said. "They'll be fine. Maria can run Nativity lines with Lily. I'll make popcorn and keep them alive."

Now six adults stood on the deck of a tour boat sliding past Newport Beach mansions glowing so brightly they looked radioactive. Nutcrackers and animatronic Santas flickered from across the water, their reflections breaking into shards of color every time the boat shifted. Cheesy carols with too much brass from a nearby yacht drifted across the waves as someone on the upper deck called "Merry Christmas!" to strangers, like holiday joy couldn't be contained to just one boat.

Caroline pressed against Darcy's side, cheek cool against his shoulder. "This is ridiculous," she whispered.

"You love it," he murmured.

Her mouth curved. "I really do."

Her hand slipped into his, warm and certain, and Darcy felt something tighten in his chest. Extravagance was worth it if it meant holding this exact moment.

A few feet away, Lucy and Eddie leaned on the rail, hands linked. Beside them, Marianne's arm looped through Rick's as she pointed toward a synchronized caroler display. Graciela, Maria's mom, snapped pictures like she was stockpiling proof to show all of her students. For a few minutes, Croft Beach and all its whispers felt far away. It was just them, laughter, and the shimmering lights turning the water into a kaleidoscope.

Until Mrs. Collins appeared.

She moved toward them like a cold wind, Priscilla and her other followers at her elbow. "Caroline. Marianne. Enjoying yourselves?"

Caroline stayed composed and her face betrayed none of her feelings as she turned to face the women from church. "Yes. It's beautiful."

Mrs. Collins folded her arms, gaze sliding toward Graciela. "It must feel… gratifying to have your *little* student chosen for such a prominent role."

"Maria?" Caroline asked.

Priscilla Jennings smiled, polite but pointed. "She's a sweet girl. Surprising, really."

Darcy's shoulders went stiff. He angled slightly, putting himself between the newcomers and his party. "Surprising how?" His voice was cool, crisp as winter air.

Mrs. Collins sighed. "Some parents feel having a girl of color as the Virgin Mary is… Well, it sends… a confusing message. My sweet Ava was devastated."

Graciela froze, camera dropping slightly. Marianne's hand tightened on Rick's arm. Even Priscilla looked shocked that her best friend would take it so far. The laughter and carols from the other side of the boat suddenly felt miles away, leaving only the bitter chill of the words hanging between them.

Eddie's voice cut through, calm but edged. "Remarkable how scandalized Croft Beach gets over inclusion. This is the 21st century."

Mrs. Collins' chin lifted. "I beg your pardon?"

Eddie gestured to the lights spilling across the bay. "Look around. Families of every background are enjoying the same holiday. No one else seems to think it's a crisis."

A friend of Mrs. Collins frowned as she listened to Pastor Eddie's impromptu sermon. "It isn't the same."

"No, it isn't," Eddie agreed, keeping a steady hand on Lucy's shoulder. "I hope you learn from this, Mrs. Simms. Out here people aren't pretending it's still the nineteenth century and I doubt you could find a verse where Jesus practiced segregation."

Angie Simms, the friend who had been called out, drew a sharp breath and pasted on a brittle smile as Mrs. Collins pulled her and the others away but not before saying a snarky goodbye.

Darcy exhaled slowly, unclenching his fists before he left half-moons in his palms. Caroline's breathing had gone shallow, her body tense against him. He pulled her closer, his arm firm around her waist, lowering his head until his lips brushed her temple.

"You okay?" he murmured.

Her laugh was small, shaky. "You know you're marrying into this circus called my life."

Darcy tipped her chin up so she couldn't look away. "I'm not marrying into it, Caroline. I'm choosing it. Choosing you. Every single time." He kissed her again, holding her there against his chest as the boat drifted past another explosion of lights. "Don't ever forget how much I love you," he murmured.

Behind them, Rick let out a dry chuckle. "Stepford Wives have nothing on Croft Beach."

Marianne muttered, "I'd take a Stepford Wife over Mrs. Collins any day."

Darcy tightened his arm around Caroline, keeping her anchored against him as the boat slid on, its holiday lights feeling less decorative now and more like a quiet declaration: we're here, we belong, and no one's taking that joy away. And as the lights shimmered across her face, Darcy thought he'd never seen anything more beautiful than a woman who refused to bow to smallness.

CHAPTER 9

Rick

By the time Maria and her mom rolled up, the house already smelled of woodsmoke and slow-cooker chili. Ellie darted down the hall with Flippers under one arm and Quackers under the other, curls bouncing as she shouted, "They're here! They're here!" like royalty had arrived instead of a friend with her sleeping bag.

Maria's mom, Graciela, stepped in first with her trademark smile. She carried a piping hot casserole dish wrapped in a couple towels. "She's been excited about this sleepover all week," she said, nodding toward Maria, who hovered shyly behind her.

"That makes two of them," Rick said, stepping back to let them in. "Lily's been talking about it nonstop."

Maria's mouth quirked, and Lily rushed in to tug her toward the den, where sleeping bags and pillows were piled high. Ellie trailed after them, dragging an oversized blanket like she was leading a parade.

Graciela's gaze swept the entryway. "Your place feels… peaceful. Feel like it is home yet?"

The word landed harder than she knew. There'd been a time when even quiet spaces felt dangerous, when four walls and a locked door meant someone else had control. Now his own walls, his own lock, his kids laughing in the next room—it felt like defiance and grace rolled into one.

Rick couldn't help laughing. "Thank you. It's definitely beginning to feel like home."

The front door opened again, and Marianne stepped inside with her elder sister, Elinor, on her heels, both shrugging off scarves and lightweight jean jackets. Marianne's face lit at the sight of Graciela. "You made it! Are Eddie and Lucy already here?"

Elinor's eyes skimmed the room and landed on Rick briefly and coolly, as if she was checking a box on a list rather than greeting him. Her handshake was polite, and her smile was tight and clipped at the edges as if she was hunting around for something nice to say. "You really do have sweet children."

"Thanks," he said, not missing how quickly her attention slid past him to Marianne. It was like he was always being weighed and found wanting without her even bothering to get to know him.

Lucy appeared from the kitchen, wiping her hands on a dish towel. "Marianne, so glad you're here."

Marianne smiled. "Elinor, this is Pastor Eddie and his wife, Lucy."

Elinor shook Lucy's hand before turning to Eddie. "Pleasure to meet you," she said, voice smooth and practiced.

"Likewise," Eddie replied, jaw tightening as he let go.

Walter's voice piped up from the hallway. "Didn't you guys meet last week? When we were moving in?"

Something flickered in Elinor's eye, but her smile didn't falter. "Oh, yes… of course. How forgetful of me."

Lucy's eyes sharply darted between them before she forced a smile. "I'll be in the kitchen. Dinner isn't going to prep itself."

Her tone had an edge now, and she disappeared toward the kitchen before anyone could answer. Caroline's jaw tightened briefly as she followed, Marianne right behind her. It was the kind of shift you felt in your bones, something unspoken that cracked the air but left no one willing to name it.

The kids could be heard having a whale of a time in the den, laughing so loudly it rattled the window panes. From their chatter, Rick caught fragments: "Ava said…" and "Kayla thinks she's so cool…" followed by Maria's soft voice: "They don't even know me." Lily's reply, sharp but protective, cut in too quiet to catch every word, but enough to know she was standing her ground.

He made a mental note to tell Lily later how proud he was she had Maria's back, then turned toward the kitchen.

Inside the kitchen, Lucy stood with her back to him, stirring the crock pot of chili a little harder than necessary while Caroline arranged rolls in a basket and Graciela grated cheese. Marianne leaned against the counter, murmuring something low, her hand resting lightly on Lucy's shoulder. Lucy didn't shrug it off, but she didn't lean into it either.

Eddie wandered in behind Rick, rubbing the back of his neck. He reached for the salad bowl just as Elinor also reached out to claim it. Their eyes met, and she smiled a second too long. Lucy saw it and set the spoon down with a clatter.

"I'm going to check on the kids," she said, voice thin, already moving toward the den.

Caroline and Marianne exchanged a quick glance, silent and telling, before they busied themselves with moving the food to the dining room.

Rick stayed by the door, watching Eddie's shoulders stiffen and Elinor's gaze drop to the floor. His stomach knotted. For a split second, the smell of chili and rolls blurred with the metallic tang of panic, too much like other rooms where tension crawled along the skin. He gripped the door frame hard until the kitchen came back into focus.

Dinner itself went smoother than expected and soon the kids were back in the den building a fort out of couch cushions as the adults tried talking too hard about safe things like holiday plans and favorite movies as they cleared the dishes. Rick however couldn't shake the image of Lucy as she'd walked out of the kitchen or the way Caroline's face had gone quiet. Whatever had just happened, it wasn't done yet.

Later, when the kids finally crashed under their blanket fort and the adults started heading home, Marianne slid her arm around Rick's waist. "Successful first sleepover," she murmured.

"So far," he agreed, glancing toward the kitchen where the dish towel Lucy had left behind still hung, twisted and damp.

She laughed softly, leading him gently outside to the backyard. "I love this place. It almost feels like you live on your own private island here with the ocean practically at your back door."

He followed her gaze out toward the moonlit waves. For years, the ocean had been a reminder of what he could not have. Now it meant freedom, possibility and the steady breath of God Himself rolling in and out, reminding him they were safe.

He sighed appreciatively before tentatively asking, "Elinor doesn't approve of me, does she?"

Marianne's smile dimmed a little. "She's... protective. Always has been. After Dad died, she practically raised Maggie while Mom grieved. And I was… well, I was me—feeling everything too much, chasing music, ignoring reality. Elinor stepped up and never really stopped—especially after Mom passed away too."

"Are she and Maggie close?"

"Maggie? She's ten going on twenty-five. I'm still surprised Elinor agreed to let her stay back home with her school friend for the Christmas break. I guess she begged until Elinor gave in."

Rick nodded, then looked back at her. "So Elinor looks at me and sees…"

"A man with kids and baggage," Marianne said quietly. "She thinks I'm signing up for heartbreak."

His jaw tightened. "She didn't think that about Willoughby, though?"

Marianne winced, then laughed softly. "No. She liked him and thought he was charming and dependable. And look how that turned out, with him having a quickie wedding to his pregnant girlfriend who wasn't me."

"Exactly my point," Rick grunted. "I'm not Willoughby."

"I know that," she said, turning around in his arms. "Elinor doesn't but she'll see you're the man for me, eventually."

Something inside him eased even as a protective spark lingered. He trailed a path of kisses down her neck. "She'll figure it out eventually. Until then…"

"Until then?" she asked, voice low.

He kissed her again, slow and certain, months of quiet moments and long patience pouring into the press of his mouth on hers. She curled her fingers into his shirt, holding him like she'd never doubted.

When they finally eased apart, he framed her face in his palms, memorizing the smooth line of her jaw and the trail of freckles across her nose he loved. "You're it, Marianne. I knew you were the one since Halloween but I think I have loved you since I first saw you walking down the steps into the basement."

Her hand slid over his heart, fingertips brushing his shirt like a note plucked on a string. "Good. Because I'm not going anywhere, Rick."

He smiled warmly, pulling his phone from his pocket and scrolling until he found what he wanted. The soft, winding melody of Prokofiev filled the night air. It was the same song she had played that had steadied his hands on a porch swing not long ago.

Marianne's eyes widened, lips parting in surprise. "Rick…"

"Dance with me," he said softly, offering his hand.

She took it without hesitation, and he drew her close. The music swelled as the waves kept time as they swayed under the stars.

For a man who had once thought joy was something he'd lost forever, the simplicity of this moment, with her head on his chest, the ocean singing harmony, and knowing his children were safe inside, felt like a prayer answered.

When the last note faded, she tipped her head back, smiling up into his grinning eyes. He kissed her again, deeper this time, until even the ocean hushed to listen.

CHAPTER 10
Darcy

The sanctuary was hushed when Darcy and his fiancée stepped inside. Two candles on the wreath near the altar waited to be lit tomorrow, wax pooling over the edges from last Sunday. The faint bite of evergreen swirled under the dry hum of heating vents.

Pastor Eddie and his wife were already seated near the front when the couple arrived. Eddie sat with one ankle crossed over his knee, perfectly casual except for the way his knuckles whitened around the manila folder in his lap. Lucy curled slightly inward, twisting her wedding band like she could spin worry into metal.

Darcy had known Eddie Ferrars long enough to recognize the difference between exhaustion and tension. Today, the tension was winning.

Caroline's hand tightened on Darcy's as they approached. She didn't paste on a polite church smile for Eddie as she bent to kiss Lucy on the cheek and gave her a look that could be interpreted as saying, *You're not alone.*

"Morning," Eddie said, a bit too quickly.

Darcy studied him a beat longer. "Everything all right?"

"Of course," Eddie said, the word clipped enough to ring false.

Caroline slid in beside Lucy. "You sure?"

Lucy's voice caught as she looked at the ground. "We talked last night."

Caroline's jaw flexed but she let it drop, which Darcy knew for her took a great deal of work.

Eddie set his folder on his knee. "Today's topic is trust," he said, forcing the professional cadence he used for premarital counseling.

Caroline let out a quiet huff. "Ironic choice."

"Caroline…" Lucy's voice was thin, almost pleading.

"No," Caroline said, chin lifting. "If you're talking about honesty and trust, maybe *you* should actually practice it."

Eddie's jaw tightened, thumb tapping once on the folder. "This isn't the time."

"Isn't it?"

Lucy twisted her ring faster, eyes shut against the weight of the moment. Darcy laid a hand on Caroline's knee with enough pressure to suggest, *not now.*

"I'm fine," Lucy whispered. Brittle.

Eddie's dropped his professional veneer as he looked at his wife intently. "Lucy?"

Lucy hesitated, eyes shiny, then whispered, "I'm hurt. But I'm still here. We can talk more later when we get home."

Something in Eddie's face faltered. Was it grief and relief colliding in one raw flash? "I love you," he said quietly.

No one moved until finally Darcy cleared his throat and suggested, "maybe we should pick this up next week."

Eddie gave a small nod, looking like a man grateful for an exit.

Outside, Caroline crossed the parking lot with her arms folded tight, eyes locked on the pavement. Darcy unlocked the car but didn't open her door. "Want to tell me what that was really about?"

She seemed to be weighing the words as she looked up at him. "Lucy came to my house last night. After Rick's chili dinner."

A cold knot formed low in Darcy's gut. "Because of Eddie?"

Caroline nodded. "She saw something—between him and Elinor."

His jaw set. "Something *what?*"

"Surely you saw the way that Eddie and Marianne's sister Elinor were looking at each other," Caroline whispered. "Obviously she hated it."

Darcy's fingers curled around the car fob. "And you think there's something going on?"

"I don't know. But I've never seen Lucy that... undone. Honestly, Darcy, I would have been sorely tempted to kill you if it had been you and Lizzie caught making eyes with each other."

He reached for her hand, threading his fingers through hers. "You'd kill me, would you?"

"I would be tempted so don't even think about it."

Darcy laughed softly as he kissed her cheek. "I'll try to walk the straight and narrow but there's something very sexy about the idea of you being jealous, darling."

She looked up, eyes sharp but wet at the edges. "I don't want this to be us," she whispered. "Promise me that years from now we will not be pretending that everything's fine when it isn't."

He tipped her chin so she had to meet his eyes. "It won't be."

"You can't know that."

"I do." His voice was quiet but certain. "For a long time I thought I already knew how my story would end with Lizzie. Everyone thought so. It felt inevitable, like the script had already been written." His thumb brushed her cheek. "But I was wrong. God's plans are better than mine, better than anyone's expectations. And His plan was you. That's why I know we won't ever settle for pretending. You are the woman He chose for me and I swear that I will never give up on us."

Her breath shuddered out as she leaned into him, forehead against his chest, arms tight around his waist. He held her there, breathing in the faint scent of the perfume from her braids and promised himself that whatever else in this town frayed, *they* wouldn't.

When she stepped back, wiping at her eyes, he said, "Come with me. One more stop."

She frowned. "Darcy... what?"

"You'll see."

The tailor shop bell chimed as they stepped inside. Caroline blinked. "A tailor?"

"I'm having a suit made," Darcy said simply. "Custom made. If you get to buy a one-of-a-kind dress, I want a suit that's a symbol to you and our guests that this is just as important to me as it is for you with your custom dress."

Her brows lifted. "You hate shopping."

"I do. But I love you more. And this isn't just about our wedding." He gestured toward the framed wedding photos on the wall. "My dad had his wedding suit made here. Mom said it was the one day she ever saw him nervous. I want to carry a part of my parents with me on our special day. They would have loved you."

Her lips parted softly. "Darcy…"

"Tell me about your mom's wedding outfit," he said, motioning for the tailor to wait.

"She wore a gorgeous white satin gown that she'd bought downtown at a little shop that specialized in gently used dresses and a *gele*—a Nigerian headwrap—in coral and gold. My dad had a classic tux. In their photos they always look to me like the happiest couple alive."

"Then let's do the same," he said. "Let's show the world *our* worlds coming together on New Year's Eve."

Caroline laughed through tears. "You're ridiculous."

"Probably," he said, brushing a knuckle under her chin. "But you love it."

Her eyes shimmered. "I do."

While the tailor measured him, Caroline wandered to the fabric table, fingers brushing over fabric swatches as she studied the wedding photo of Darcy's parents. By the time he stepped off the platform, some of the weight from church had lifted from her shoulders.

Darcy stepped behind her, sliding a hand to her waist. She turned, and he kissed her slow, unhurried, letting the taste of peppermint from her lip balm linger.

She smiled, cheeks warm. "You and your surprises."

"Get used to them," he said, kissing her again until her smile deepened against his mouth.

CHAPTER 11

Rick

Rick had been to the Christmas tree lot more times than he could count. Every December since moving to Croft Beach when he was five years old, he and his mom would come on the first weekend, hot cider in hand, and argue over the perfect Christmas tree and laugh at trees too big to ever fit through their apartment door.

He never thought he'd be back here years later, holding his daughter's mittened hand, picking a tree for *his* family.

Three-year-old Ellie darted ahead, boots crunching on loose needles. "Daddy, look at this one!" She hugged a squat noble fir that was roughly her size.

Sam wrinkled his nose. "That's a baby tree."

Ellie stuck out her tongue. "It's cute."

Marianne chuckled, tucking Lily's scarf snug. Elinor walked alongside her sister, quiet and watchful, her eyes lingering on the kids as though she was still figuring out how to fit into this new chapter of Marianne's life.

"Look how tall this tree is," Lily whispered, eyes wide as she stared up at a Douglas fir that had to be ten feet high.

"Some are taller," Rick said, crouching slightly. "What do you think?"

She picked up a fallen branch, turning it over carefully. "It's... a lot."

Marianne crouched beside her. "This is your first Christmas tree lot, isn't it?"

Lily nodded, voice hushed. "I've only ever seen Christmas trees in pictures."

Rick's chest tightened. *No kid should have to say that.* He touched her shoulder gently. "It's okay to like it, Sweetheart. This is ours now. Our new tradition."

Ellie called from two rows over, hugging a tree twice her size. "This one is special!"

Sam groaned. "You can't pick all of them, Ellie."

Ellie ignored him and clung to her prize. "Daddy, *please?*"

Rick scooped her up, breathing in her lavender scented shampoo. "Special wins," he said.

"Rick Wentworth? Oh, it *is* you!"

Miss Bates bustled toward him, cider cup in one hand, tote bag swinging wildly. "I told Priscilla Jennings, 'That's Rick Wentworth, back safe and sound, praise the Lord!' and she said, 'It *is* him,' and I said, 'Well, I simply must say hello!' Oh, and look at these children—*precious!* And your home, I heard about it, such a blessing—why, your mother would be so proud, Rick, so proud."

Rick smiled, shifting Ellie on his hip. "Good to see you, Miss Bates."

She beamed at Marianne, at Elinor, at every child within range, then bustled off toward another victim of her enthusiasm.

Marianne slid her hand into Rick's as he set Ellie down. "You okay?"

He nodded. "Better than okay."

Rick couldn't help but laugh. *Better than last year?* Last year couldn't even compare. What kind of Christmas could he call last year with their paper drawings of Christmas trees in Louisa's cellar and his reluctant agreement to let Louisa use his body in the hopes that she would show some kindness to Lily with a new book for Christmas.

Several hours later, the tree Ellie had chosen stood crooked but proud in the corner while Rick wrestled with the box of white lights he'd bought at the hardware store.

"It's crooked," Ellie observed solemnly.

"I know."

"You should ask Uncle Darcy for help," she suggested.

"I'm fine," he muttered.

The doorbell rang, and suddenly the house filled with people. Marianne and Elinor carried in fragrant takeout, Darcy held a tin of cookies, Caroline was in possession of a box full of brightly colored babbles for the tree, and Eddie and Lucy trailed close behind with a couple bottles of apple cider. Lucy's smile was tight, her eyes flicking briefly toward Elinor before she ducked into the kitchen with Marianne.

Darcy surveyed the tree like it was a courtroom exhibit. "Want help before you strangle yourself?"

"No."

"Too bad." He shrugged out of his coat and grabbed the lights. "Eddie, you're on ladder duty."

"I nearly electrocuted myself putting up church lights," Eddie said dryly.

"That explains a lot," Darcy muttered, already untangling the cord.

Caroline angled for a photo. "Smile, everyone! This one is going in the scrapbook."

Sam opened a storage box. "Look at our ornaments!"

Lily proudly held up a felt lion. "Uncle Darcy, I named him Darcy because you gave me Leo the Lion."

Darcy crouched, eyes soft. "That's one beautiful lion. Thank you, Sweetheart."

Ellie shoved a penguin ornament at Caroline. "Look what I picked!"

Caroline crouched, smoothing Ellie's hair. "Sweetest penguin I've ever seen."

"Ava said only poor kids buy ornaments like these," Lily turned and whispered to Maria who rolled her eyes.

Maria's mouth twisted. "Kayla Jennings said that too. They're mean. Anyway, they don't even decorate their own trees. Their maids do."

The girls giggled and went back to hanging ornaments, and Rick filed away the comment for later.

By the time the lights blinked steady, the house smelled like pine and orange chicken, laughter echoing off every wall. Even his next-door neighbor George Knightley had shown up sometime before dinner and was now smiling as Sam proudly showed him a soccer ball ornament he'd chosen at the craft fair the school held.

"Do you have any Christmas morning plans?" George asked the group at large during a lull in the conversation.

"I've been pestered Rick and the kids to come to my house," Darcy grinned. "It's been so empty and quiet ever since they moved in here."

"Move in with us!" Ellie giggled as she walked over and gave him a loud kiss on the cheek before plopping down on Caroline's lap.

"Actually, I was hoping you all would come over Christmas morning," Rick shared as he looked in the corner where the tree now proudly stood. "It'll be the first Christmas I can spend with all of my children and the first Christmas in a decade since Louisa…" A quick look at his children's faces had Rick coughing and changing his comment mid-sentence. "Well, you know… anyway, it'll be special to be here in our new house and I'd love for you all to join us."

Caroline smiled broadly at him as she squeezed Ellie close. "We wouldn't miss it as long as you don't mind my possibly bringing my cousin Tabitha and her husband Jordan too. They are due to fly in for the wedding sometime before Christmas."

Rick grinned and nodded his agreement as others threw out suggestions and thoughts about Christmas morning traditions and plans.

When the guests had finally gone for the night and the kids had fallen asleep in their respective beds, Rick stepped outside. The sand was cool, the waves visible under a nearly full moon.

Marianne stood barefoot in the dunes, shoes dangling from one hand, hair loose in the sea breeze.

He slipped an arm around her waist. "Last Christmas, I had no idea that in just two months I'd be seeing a gorgeous Korean American angel walk down the cellar steps to come rescue Lily and me."

Her fingers traced the line of his jaw. "I thank God daily that I got the call to the Elliot Estate that night."

Rick, sensing she was about to start crying at the thought of what she'd seen in the cellar, kissed her reverently as the salt air curled around them. She rose on her toes, fingers sliding into his hair, kissing him as if she'd always been waiting for this exact moment.

When they pulled back, she whispered against his mouth, "Wow."

He smiled, thumb brushing her cheek. "Stealing the word right from me."

Her answering laugh was quiet, sweet, and full of promise.

CHAPTER 12

Darcy

Caroline's hand was warm in Darcy's, their fingers held tight with quiet certainty, as parishioners spilled into the church courtyard, laughter and choir music trailing out the sanctuary doors.

He could not deny that he had spent most of the sermon watching Caroline. He had seen her eyes closed in prayer, lips moving silently, shoulders steady with that quiet strength she carried like armor and grace at once. Sometimes like today it still hit him, sharp and surreal, that this woman was his future.

Then he saw Lucy.

She stood near the bulletin board, clipboard clutched to her chest, facing Mrs. Collins and her pastel entourage—the Croft Beach Inquisition. Darcy tensed, ready to step in, but Lucy lifted her chin first.

"I understand your concerns about casting," she said evenly. "But if you'd like to help, there are costumes that need sewing."

"Sewing?" Mrs. Collins blinked.

"Yes. Angel robes need hemming. Shepherd costumes need seams reinforced. I can sign you up now."

Angie Simms, one of Mrs. Collins' minions, seemed to never know when to hold her tongue as she blurted out. "I've never sewn a thing in my life."

Lucy didn't flinch. "It's never too late to learn."

Beside Darcy, Caroline's shoulders shook, eyes bright with suppressed laughter.

Mrs. Collins hesitated, muttered something about *looking at the sign-up sheet*, and retreated with Angie and her other friends. Lucy sagged slightly, exhaustion breaking through her composure.

Darcy stepped forward. "You handled that beautifully."

Her cheeks flushed. "Mrs. Collins terrifies me."

"I think she terrifies everyone. Have you ever wondered why no one calls her by her first name?"

"I don't even know her first name," Caroline laughed as she tucked her hand into Darcy's arm. "Do you know it?"

"Nope," Darcy replied with a wink for his future wife before turning back to Lucy. "But for the record, you didn't look terrified."

With a grateful smile, Lucy turned to the kids and clapped her hands raised her clipboard. "Places, please! Let's try the shepherd scene first with our Angel of the Lord bringing the good news."

Ellie marched to the front, her halo crooked, and jaw set like a gladiator walking into battle. She lifted her arms dramatically.

"BEHOLD— I AM THE ANGEL OF THE LORD!" she bellowed, voice echoing off the rafters.

Two shepherd boys flinched so hard they nearly dropped their crooks. Rick pinched the bridge of his nose to keep from laughing out loud.

"FEAR NOT! FOR I BRING YOU GOOD TIDINGS OF…"
Ellie squinted at the back of the sanctuary as if for inspiration, then
yelled, "…HAPPY STUFF!"

A shepherd whispered something to his friend. Ellie stomped over
and snatched his staff, and hollered, "SILENCE, SHEEP BOY! I
AM THE ANGEL!"

Lucy half squeaked, half gasped. "Ellie, honey, maybe—"

"YOU WILL FIND THE BABY JESUS… IN A BOX!" Ellie
boomed triumphantly.

Caroline collapsed into the pew, tears of laughter streaming down
her face.

Mrs. Collins hissed from the doorway, "She's threatening the
shepherds with a staff!"

"She most certainly is and my beautiful Caitlin is up there," Priscilla
Jennings sniffed, clutching her pearls like her daughter really was in
danger of Ellie.

Ellie, caring nothing of the adult drama happening off-stage,
stabbed the air with the purloined staff. "AND GLORY TO…
EVERYBODY, EVERYWHERE, FOR ALL TIME!"

Her halo slid over one eye like a pirate patch as she spun in a circle
doing jazz hands. The shepherds muttered their lines in defeat as
Rick groaned into his hands.

"She gets this from you," he muttered to Darcy.

"Absolutely," Darcy said, grinning so hard his cheeks hurt.

Lucy's desperate eyes darted toward them. He couldn't help laughing even harder as he declared, "this will be the most unforgettable Nativity Croft Beach has ever seen."

Ellie beamed like she'd just conquered Rome.

By the time he left for John Wayne Airport, the laughter had faded to a tightness in Darcy's chest. His younger sister Georgie's text—*landed, baggage claim*—still buzzed on his phone when she came barreling toward him: all long limbs, flowing hair, and a grin that stole his breath the same way it always had.

"You grew again," he muttered, still finding it hard to believe his sister was no longer a kid but now a sophomore in college.

"You look older," she shot back, smiling.

Then he saw who was behind her.

Lizzie Bennet Wickham.

Her chin tipped high, eyes steady but unreadable. For a split second, he felt eighteen again. He was the uncertain, foolish boy who thought Lizzie's dancing gray eyes were worth everything.

"Surprise!" Georgie beamed, practically vibrating. "We sat together the whole flight. She's divorced now!"

Blood drained from Darcy's face.

Lizzie's mouth curved faintly. "Hello, Darcy."

"Lizzie," he said hoarsely.

"She's staying at the house!" Georgie announced, glowing like she'd just orchestrated world peace. "You have, like, a hundred bedrooms."

"Seven," he muttered.

"Exactly," Georgie said, triumphant. "Perfect for Christmas."

Lizzie smiled sweet and sharp. "I don't want to impose—"

"You wouldn't be imposing," Georgie cut in. "Right, Darcy?"

God help him.

"Fine," he muttered, because Georgie was acting like it was a done deal.

The drive back felt like every muscle in his body had locked tight. Lizzie sat angled toward him, smelling of the same citrus-and-soap scent he'd spent years trying to forget. Georgie filled the silence, recounting his and Lizzie's college romance like it was some golden-age love story, each word driving Caroline's face into his mind like a blade.

He began to understand why people might joke about selling their soul to get out of something as he dearly wanted to escape and to skip the next stop when Georgie begged to go to Priscilla Jennings' bakery. And that's where it got worse.

Caroline sat at a corner table with Lucy, Marianne, and Elinor, laughing over tea and scones until she saw Lizzie.

Her hand froze on her teacup. Lucy went rigid, Marianne's brows arched high, and Elinor sipped her tea like she was watching a car crash in slow motion.

Georgie bounded over. "Hi! You remember Lizzie, right? Darcy's ex? She's divorced now and staying with us for the holidays!"

The silence was so sharp it hurt. Caroline's knuckles whitened around her cup.

Priscilla Jennings bustled up from behind the counter, delighted. "Elizabeth Bennet! It was such a tragedy when you left Darcy for that sly boy Wickham! I always said you and Darcy were a match made in Heaven."

Lizzie smiled as she hugged the older woman. "Maybe I made a mistake letting him go."

Darcy couldn't breathe. He opened his mouth, searching for words, but nothing came. He took the coward's path out, bolting and texting Rick an SOS but it was George Knightley who called him instead.

"Darcy? Why are you texting me in all caps?"

"I panicked," he muttered, already leaving the bakery. "I thought I was texting Rick. You won't believe what's happened in the last couple of hours."

"Try me," George said, opening his front door as Darcy arrived.

"Where to even begin? My ex-girlfriend is back in town. My kid sister is trying to play matchmaker. Priscilla Jennings looked ready to toast our freaking history. Lizzie said she might've made a mistake letting me go. And that's not even the worst!"

"Worst? How does it get any worse?"

"Caroline was in the bakery when we all walked in! Now do you see why I sent the SOS text?"

Darcy could practically *feel* the disapproval radiating from George's silence before he finally asked, "How did you let this happen?"

"I don't know."

George's voice was calm steel. "You better figure it out quickly. This isn't about Lizzie or Caroline. It's about you deciding who you are and not letting old history destroy your future."

Two hours later, after driving around restlessly once he'd left George's place, Darcy parked in front of Caroline's house. Her home smelled faintly of vanilla and lemongrass and heartbreak. She sat rigid on the couch, nails digging into her palm to keep from shaking, hands folded tight.

"I'm sorry," he said finally.

Her brow arched. "For which part?"

He rubbed his face. "For running out of the bakery like a coward. For shutting off my phone. For not warning you Lizzie was back. For letting Georgie talk me into hosting my ex-girlfriend. I should've said no."

"Does the fact that Lizzie is single again change your plans to marry me?" she asked quietly.

The question hit like a gut punch. He hesitated and she saw it.

"Do you know what the worst part was?" she sighed. "Sitting there while Lizzie, your sister, and Priscilla Jennings all looked at me like I was an intruder in your life."

"Caroline—"

"They reminded me Lizzie is Croft Beach royalty. The girl everyone expected you to marry. White. Pretty. Safe. Yes, I was a jerk in college but I'm sick and tired of feeling like second best. In their eyes I will always be the girl you noticed only after Lizzie Bennet broke up with you."

"You're not second best. I love you."

"I know you love me but is it enough? Do you want me enough to stand with me when Lizzie is offering herself up to you on a silver platter?"

"Please," he whispered. "Let me stay. We can talk. Or sit. Something."

She cupped his cheek, hand trembling. He covered it, leaned in, brushed his mouth over hers. The kiss was desperate, full of everything he couldn't put into words. When she finally drew back, her breath was uneven.

"I love you," she whispered.

"I love you more," he murmured.

She stepped back, voice quiet but firm. "But I need space."

The words cut deeper than any argument. He nodded, because fighting would only make it worse, and left.

Outside, the cold hit him like a wave. He sat in the driver's seat but didn't start the engine, staring at his hands on the steering wheel until they blurred behind the sheen of tears. His chest tightened, a hollowness so deep it felt bottomless. Caroline's taste was still on his lips, her scent clinging to his shirt, but the seat beside him was empty, and for the first time in years, he felt like a man who'd been handed the whole world and still managed to drop it.

CHAPTER 13

Rick

The kitchen smelled like burnt coffee and cold Chinese food. Rick stood at the counter, hands wrapped around a mug he hadn't actually drunk from, watching steam curl and fade like the day itself.

In the living room, Caroline sat curled against Marianne, shoulders shaking in exhausted silence. Marianne held her close, eyes raw when they lifted to meet his.

The kids were already in bed, worn out from sugar and too much tension they didn't understand. Rick was grateful the children had been spared the adult version of Christmas chaos.

His phone buzzed on the counter. Darcy.

Rick sighed, rubbing a hand over his face before answering. "Yeah." His voice came out hoarse.

There was a pause, then Darcy's voice—ragged, heavy. "Rick."

Rick leaned back against the counter, eyes shutting briefly. "Yeah, I'm here."

The line crackled softly. "I sent her to a hotel."

"Hotel?" For a second, Rick thought he'd misheard. "Who?"

"Lizzie," Darcy breathed. "I told her she couldn't stay with me. Georgie's furious. She took her there herself."

Rick exhaled slow, glancing at Caroline still clinging to Marianne like the last rope on a fraying dock.

"You did what you thought was right," Rick said quietly.

Darcy didn't answer.

"I need you to tell me I did the right thing," he whispered finally, voice breaking.

Rick's chest tightened. "I don't know if I can," he admitted. "I'm not sure there's a perfect move here. But... not pretending it didn't matter? Not ignoring how it made Caroline feel? That's better than letting Lizzie stay."

Another pause. "Yeah," Darcy murmured eventually.

"I'm sorry," Rick said, because it was the only honest thing left.

"Me too," Darcy whispered.

They stayed on the line, breathing through a silence that wasn't really empty.

"You sure you want to sit there all night?" Rick asked finally.

Darcy huffed something that was almost a laugh. "What else am I supposed to do?"

"You could come here," Rick said. "Talk it out face to face. Caroline is here. She came over just as Marianne was leaving and is pretty upset. Maybe she'd rather hear it straight from you than from anyone else."

He heard the hesitation in his best friend's voice. "I don't know if she wants to see me. She asked for space."

"Probably not," Rick admitted as he watched Caroline nod signaling her openness to seeing Darcy. "But maybe that's not the point. It's three in the morning and I want to go to bed so how about you come and win back your future wife and then all of you can leave me alone in peace because in three hours my children will be up and bouncing off the walls."

Darcy chuckled. "Rick," Darcy said after a long pause, "you think it matters to her? That I grew up with my family name, in a house like mine, while she didn't? That this town never lets her forget it?"

"You mean the working-class thing," Rick said carefully, though they both knew he meant more.

"And the fact she's Nigerian American," Darcy added quietly. "That Croft Beach looks at her and sees a florescent sign saying *not from here*. Sometimes I'm not sure I'm doing enough to stand between her and all that ugliness."

"I think it matters that you see it," Rick said slowly. "That you don't pretend it's not there. What's more, it matters that you love her in a way that doesn't make her feel like she has to become someone else to deserve it."

Darcy was silent, but the line stayed open.

"And if you're afraid you're not doing enough," Rick added, "that's probably the best sign that you are trying. Don't beat yourself up, man. I'll never forget the way you stood up for me time and time again growing up because I was the apartment dwelling scholarship kid at school whose dad died in a county hospital. You care more than most people. You just have to show it."

After another long silence, Darcy said, "I'm coming over. Just… tell her I'm on my way."

Rick looked at Caroline, who hadn't moved except to crumble another used tissue on a pile of similarly distressed Kleenex.

"She'll be here," he promised.

They hung up.

In the living room, Caroline raised her head, eyes red but sharp.

"He's on his way," Rick stated the obvious as he moved back into the living room.

"What did he say?" she asked finally, voice tight.

Marianne turned too, curious and cautious.

Rick hesitated. "He needed someone to talk to," he said carefully. "That's all."

"Rick." Her voice carried warning and weary accusation all at once.

He lifted both palms. "I'm not taking sides. That's between you and him. But I will say this—he loves you with everything he has and when he loves someone he gives them his all."

Caroline's throat worked, but she didn't reply.

"Maybe Croft Beach was never going to be perfect," Rick said gently. "From experience, I know how small minded this town can be but, Caroline, you don't have to let its narrowness destroy what you two have. That would mean that the Mrs. Collinses of the world would win."

Her eyes glistened again. "What if I'm just exhausted from always feeling like I am constantly having to prove something?"

"Then maybe that's the cost of building something real here," he said quietly. "But you're worth it. Both of you are."

Marianne rubbed Caroline's shoulder, her voice soft but steady. "You deserve to be loved out loud, Caroline. Get Darcy to tell you what he's feeling and thinking."

A tear slid down Caroline's cheek as she gripped Marianne's hand tighter.

Rick crouched so they were eye level. "Whatever you decide," he told her, "just know you're not second best. Not to him. Not to any of us. We're a motley crew, but if you'll have us, you'll never face life alone. Darcy is the brother I never had and the children, especially Ellie, would be devastated if you weren't here."

For a long moment, the only sound was the distant hum of florescent lights over the sink.

When Caroline excused herself to freshen up, Rick's eyes slid to Marianne and pride caught in his throat.

"You're a good friend," he said quietly, voice low but certain. "Stronger than most people realize. I'm proud of you."

Her eyes softened, but she only said, "Where else would I be?"

Sighing, Rick reached for her, fingers brushing the back of her neck, drawing her gently to her feet. Marianne stepped into his embrace without hesitation, her hands sliding up his chest.

Rick's voice dropped. "Do you have any idea what you do to me?"

Her answering smile was quiet, knowing. "Show me."

He kissed her—slow at first, then deeper with her arms circled around his neck. Her lips were warm, and she yielded to him with a soft sound that hit him low below his belt.

Rick lowered her back toward the couch, a hand splayed over the small of her back. Marianne's fingers curled into his shirt, pulling him closer. He kissed her like a man who'd been starving too long, like she was the one safe place in a night full of sharp edges.

When he finally drew back, his forehead rested against hers, breath rough. "You wreck me, you know that?"

Her laugh was soft, shaky. "Good."

He kissed her once more before reluctantly letting her go. "Come on. Caroline needs you," he whispered, even though part of him wanted to lock the world out and keep her right there.

Marianne smoothed her hair and nodded, slipping down the hall to check on Caroline. Rick watched her go, heat still coiled under his ribs, and thought—not for the first time—how lucky he was to have her in his life.

CHAPTER 14

Darcy

Rick opened the door, but Darcy hardly registered him.

Caroline slowly walked into the room from the hall and when she looked up at him, the rest of the room vanished.

"You," he said, voice catching before he could stop it. "You're the only thing that matters."

Caroline walked slowly forward into the room, shoulders squared like she was bracing for impact, and walked right past him. Shock clouded his mind for a second before he followed her out the back door, down the wooden footpath toward the water. Strings of white lights strung overhead caught in her braids, silver threads glinting as she folded her arms and stared at the dark surf.

"Say what you came to say," she murmured.

Darcy swallowed hard. "When Lizzie showed up…" He exhaled, rough and unsteady. "All it did was prove I don't want that life anymore. I want you."

She still didn't look at him. "I don't need you to save me, Darcy."

"I know."

Her gaze lifted, raw and luminous. "Then why does it still feel like you're trying?"

He stepped closer—not to corner her, but so she could see all of him. "Because I love you, Caroline. And I don't know how to love you small."

A tear slid down her cheek.

"I'm tired," she whispered. "Tired of walking into rooms and feeling like I have to prove I'm enough."

"You never have to prove that to me," he said softly. "Not once. Not ever."

Her mouth trembled.

"I don't love you because you're different," he continued, voice steady now. "I love you because you're *you*—the strongest, kindest, most brilliant person I know. And I'm humbled every day that you let me love you at all."

Her eyes closed, shoulders shaking.

"If tomorrow you want me to walk back into Croft Beach and tell them all they don't get a vote on our happy ending?" he said. "I will. And if you don't want to stay, we leave and we go to wherever you want to go. You know why? You are my home, Caroline—not this town."

Her breath shuddered.

"And if someday you want to come back," he added, quieter now, "we'll walk in together, head high. You are not a compromise. You are not second choice. You are the greatest honor of my life."

She covered her mouth, eyes bright. "You keep saying you hate how I feel, but you don't really understand it."

He nodded slowly. "You're right. I don't. I've been judged for my name, for my money—but never for merely existing in a room and for looking different. I don't know that weight. I won't pretend I do."

Her chin trembled.

"But if you'll let me," he said, stepping closer, "I'll stand with you every single time it happens. And I'll never be the one who makes you question if you're enough."

Her voice wavered. "And if someday you're tired of the fight?"

"Then I'll still be here. Because loving you isn't a fight—it's the only thing I want to do."

Her arms unfolded, resting flat against his chest. He brushed his thumbs over her damp cheeks and lowered his head, slow as a prayer. The kiss was soft at first, then deepened when she rose onto her toes to meet him halfway. Her hands fisted in his shirt, clinging like she'd finally let go of every wall she'd been holding up. The kiss shifted—urgent, then steady, an unspoken vow sealed against her lips.

When he pulled back, their foreheads rested together, breath mingling in the cool night air. Peace flickered in her eyes for the first time all evening.

"Okay," she whispered.

Darcy let out a shaky breath, catching one of her braids and sliding it between his fingers, reverent. "You carry beauty into rooms that don't know how to hold it," he said softly. "And I will never stop seeing it."

Her laugh was small and wet, but real. "That's… worth everything."

He kissed the crown of her head, letting the braid slip free. "No," he whispered. "*You're* worth everything."

CHAPTER 15

Rick

Rick had no idea what Darcy meant by "a conversation," only that Caroline had twisted her engagement ring until it nearly spun off her finger and Marianne had gripped his hand under the table like she was bracing for bad news.

Eddie and Lucy sat on the couch, too close and yet too quiet with Lucy staring at the floor and Eddie staring into the middle of the room like a man waiting for the executioner. The air felt tight, heavy, like a courtroom before the judge walks in.

Darcy's front door finally opened and Darcy breezed in, followed by two people Rick hadn't seen in ages: Pastor Ned Bertram and his wife, Fanny Price-Bertram.

Marianne's breath caught. "Oh my goodness…"

Fanny's warm smile landed like a soft blanket on the room, but Ned looked thinner and paler as if carrying a quiet gravity.

Caroline jumped up and hugged Fanny tight. "What are you doing here?"

"Answering a call," Fanny grinned as she returned the hug.

Darcy explained, "I asked them to come."

Ned lifted a hand, voice steady. "It's good to see you all, although I wish it were under better circumstances."

Caroline hesitated. "What circumstances?"

Ned's fingers laced with Fanny's. "I know you were all a bit confused about our sudden retirement. Well… The reason we retired and moved earlier is because I have cancer. I've been in treatment for months but my pride refused to share that with the congregation and you all."

The room froze. Lucy's hand flew to her mouth. Caroline's eyes brimmed. Marianne's grip on Rick's hand tightened. Rick himself felt as if the earth had catapulted him into the unknown after so much peace.

"I'm not afraid," Ned said quietly. "God's carried me too far for fear to win now. But I wanted you to know the truth."

Fanny stroked her husband's hand. "When Darcy called and asked us to come pray with you, we didn't hesitate and decided this was the perfect time for us to come forth with the truth too."

"You didn't have to—" Rick began.

"We did," Fanny said gently. "Because we love you. All of you."

Ned's gaze swept the room as he took a seat on the sofa Darcy led him to. "Some of you wonder if wounds like yours can heal. If you can move forward without losing yourselves. So let me tell you something you might not know about us."

He paused, eyes soft. "When Fanny was fifteen, she came to live with my parents. She was what you'd call a foster kid. Because her family had fallen on hard times she needed a new home and since her mother worked as a cleaner for my dad at the mayor's office, it seemed to make sense that Dad would bring her into our household. But in a town like Croft Beach… you can imagine the whispers and the not so quiet comments."

"Even though I was white," Fanny added. "It didn't matter. I was still that girl. I was the poor girl, the daughter of a cleaner, and people thought I wasn't good enough for the mayor's family let alone to be courted by the mayor's son."

Caroline stiffened slightly, breath catching.

"When we started courting," Ned said, "people whispered I was throwing away my future. That she'd never fit in. That marrying her would mark me forever. But marrying her was the best choice I ever made." His smile softened. "And when God joins two people, He doesn't ask the neighborhood committee for permission."

Caroline let out a shaky laugh-sob, and Darcy reached for her hand.

"We know what it is like," Fanny said gently, "to build a life people don't approve of."

Ned's eyes locked on Darcy. "And tell me—who decided Miss Elizabeth Bennet was the better woman for you? I'd like names so I can pray over them personally."

Darcy blinked as Caroline burst out laughing through tears, covering her face. Even Eddie cracked a grin.

"You'll be up all night with half the town," Darcy muttered.

"Think I can't handle it?" Ned asked with a twinkle. "You don't owe anyone an explanation for loving the woman you do. And you," he turned to Caroline, "are not a second-best bride. You are the woman God placed in this man's life on purpose. That's not up for debate."

Caroline's chin trembled as she leaned forward to kiss the older man's cheek.

"You deserve your own happy ending," Ned said softly, "one built on faith, truth and not old expectations."

Caroline reached for Darcy's hand, fingers intertwining.

Fanny clasped Caroline's other hand. "I remember you at eighteen coming to the college group at church in order to follow Darcy around and give Lizzie headaches. You're not that girl anymore. You became someone who let God write a new story for yourself and it's one of grace and strength forged in hard places. Caroline Bingley, nothing about you is a mistake."

Caroline didn't bother to wipe away the tears that started flowing down her cheeks.

Fanny sat down next to Caroline and bundled her into a hug as she asked softly, "If you could tell us one truth about what it is like to be standing in your shoes, what would it be?"

"I'd say—," Caroline drew a breath, "that I'm not ashamed of who I am. I am proud to be my father's daughter and also my mother's and proud to be the future Mrs. Darcy. The one thing that always makes me feel small is how fast others are to judge that I am not enough for my role in your life, Darcy. Sometimes, it's hard to believe you're really loved when so many voices say you're just the consolation prize and second-best bride option. This town will always believe Darcy is destined to marry Elizabeth Bennet and I cannot help but resent that I am not even given a chance to prove how good I am for this man I love."

Her eyes locked onto Darcy's. "I don't want pity. I don't need rescuing. I just want to know that when I stand beside you, you're not wishing I was someone else."

Darcy gently brushed a tear from her cheek. "Never someone else."

Fanny turned to Marianne with a gentle smile. "And you?"

Marianne hesitated, fingers twisting together. "I spent years trying to prove I was enough but, kind of like Caroline, the neighborhood I grew up in decided I was never Korean enough nor white enough to check any boxes. And now, I feel like that in starting over here in Croft Beach, I have to prove it all over again. And—" her voice faltered. "I worry, even though what she did was so evil and perverted, that I'll never erase Louisa's hold on Rick and the kids. She was there first. What if part of him always belongs to her? What if I'm just… the safe choice?"

Next up was Lucy whose voice trembled as she confessed her own fears of never feeling like she measured up to the perfect, polished Croft Beach wife and wondering if Eddie ever noticed how much she needed him. Eddie caught her hand, looking gutted, and whispered, "I see only you."

When Ned called the men to speak, Darcy and Eddie went first owning their failures and fears and naming their love out loud.

Then all eyes landed on Rick.

"The truest thing I know?" His voice was low, rough. "That I don't know if I'll ever feel normal again." He rubbed unconsciously at the faint scar along his neck. "I still hear Louisa sometimes, like a shadow, whispering I'm broken and not good enough for Marianne or even for my own children. But I'm trying to believe God didn't make a mistake keeping me alive. That maybe I still have something to give. Marianne, you and my kids and our friends in this room are why I believe in hope again."

Marianne's tears spilled freely as she whispered, "You're my hope too."

Pastor Ned prayed, his voice steady and warm, wrapping them all in something heavier than words and lighter than fear.

Later that night, while Lily read Ellie a bedtime story and the boys constructed a fort out of blankets in their bedroom, Rick found Marianne on the porch. Barefoot, arms wrapped tight around herself, she stared into the darkness.

"You okay?" he asked softly.

She wiped her cheeks. "A little raw. But also… lighter."

He stepped close, tucking a strand of hair behind her ear. "Remember what I said at Darcy's tonight? It wasn't for show. You're everything I want, Marianne. Louisa has no place in-between us. It is just us and the children."

Her breath caught, a quiet sound of relief.

Rick pressed a soft kiss to the freckles he loved, then lowered his mouth to hers in something slow and certain, lingering until her fingers uncurled and her body melted against him. When they parted, he murmured, "Come check on the kids with me."

This time, when she slid her fingers into his, there was no hesitation at all.

CHAPTER 16

Darcy

The sanctuary was bustling with anticipation and chaos when Darcy walked in to see how the last nativity rehearsal was progressing.

Lucy Ferrars stood near the piano, clutching her clipboard like it was the only thing keeping her upright as she whispered something to Caroline Bingley who was busy fixing halos on the little angel choir participants. "All right—shepherds to the left, angels to the right, wise men center stage." Her voice was small but steady.

Ellie skipped across the platform, tinsel halo slipping sideways, then patted the doll in the manger with grave sincerity. "Hi, baby Jesus," she whispered.

Rick smiled up at his friend when Darcy slid into the pew beside him. "Pray for us."

Darcy bit back a laugh. "Your little one is committed. I'll give her that."

Staring at his best friend's peaceful face for a moment, Darcy pulled an envelope out of his pocket and handed it over. "I think you're ready to have this."

Before Rick could ask him about it, Sam and Walter marched past the men with Sam's paper crown tilted over one eyebrow and Walter's tunic dragging like he thought he was actual royalty.

Pastor Fanny leaned over from the pew behind the men, her eyes warm with memory. "They remind me of you two at that age."

Rick groaned. "Don't remind me."

From next to his wife, Pastor Ned chuckled. "If I remember correctly, you were the wise men who knocked over not only the lectern but also the manger."

"And I said something unrepeatable when I dropped the gold," Rick muttered.

Darcy lifted a brow. "In our defense, no one should trust sixth grade boys with breakable props."

From the front, Lucy called, "Wise men, please show us your gift presentation."

Sam stepped forward with solemn gravity. "We bring gold—"

Walter held up his jar. "And frankincense—"

Sam frowned. "And myrrh which is for... um..."

Walter shrugged. "Dead people."

Sam nodded seriously. "Yeah. For dead people."

The room went still.

Ellie wrinkled her nose. "That's icky."

Lucy clamped a hand over her mouth to hide her laugh. "Actually," she said gently, "those gifts were very special. Even when Jesus was born, God already knew how His life would end, and what it would mean for all of us."

A quiet hush fell over the room. Maria, shy but determined in her blue robe, reached for the doll in the manger, brushing its cheek reverently.

Walter tilted his head. "So… it's like a promise?"

Lucy nodded. "Exactly. A promise that His life, His death and resurrection was a gift."

The moment held, fragile and beautiful.

Then Mrs. Collins' voice sliced through it. "Oh, Lucy, dear, why haven't you cast a third wise man? You can't possibly expect my sweet Ava to be a shepherd without any lines when she was the star last year. It's a disgrace that you haven't bothered to cast a full nativity scene."

Lucy's smile wobbled. "Actually, Scripture never says there were three—just wise men from the East. People assume three because of the number of gifts."

Darcy had to choke back a laugh when Rick muttered, "And thus concludes the theological debate."

Mrs. Jennings chose that moment to speak up from where she sat next to Mrs. Collins and their cohorts, voice sugar-coated but sharp. "It would be confusing for the congregation not to have three."

Lucy's tone stayed polite but trembled slightly. "Thank you for your feedback, Priscilla." Lucy drew a steady breath. "Okay, children, take a quick cookie break before we run the final song."

Sam and Walter bolted for snacks, arguing over whether myrrh smelled bad since it was for dead people.

Ellie lingered by the manger, then called out, "Miss Caroline?"

Caroline crossed the room from where she'd been standing with Lucy. "Yes, Darling?"

Ellie touched one of Caroline's braid affectionately. "You look like a real angel. When I go to Heaven, I hope I look just like you."

Caroline froze, breath catching, eyes glistening. She crouched to Ellie's level, voice soft but certain. "You know what I hope? I hope that you always know you're already beautiful just the way God made you."

"Okay!" Ellie grinned. "Can we go get a cookie?"

A ripple of laughter warmed the room until Mrs. Collins gave a brittle little chuckle. "Oh, bless her heart. Surely she'd rather look like her own mama one day. It's sweet she admires you, Caroline, but it's… a little confusing, isn't it? Wanting to look like someone who looks so… different."

One of Mrs. Collins' followers flinched, eyes darting to Caroline and away again.

Caroline's hand stilled on Ellie's cheek. Her spine straightened, voice calm but unwavering. "There's nothing confusing about kindness. Ellie can look up to anyone she chooses. I'm honored she's chosen me and I love her as if she were my own."

Something tightened in Darcy's chest where he sat with Rick. Was it fierce pride? Perhaps it was regret that he hadn't spoken first. His hands curled into fists against his thighs, jaw set as Pastor Ned stepped forward, voice firm.

"Augusta, that was unkind and untrue."

The woman's sugary smile faltered most likely in shock that Pastor Ned would dare to address her by her first name. Even her husband, Pastor Collins, shifted uncomfortably where he stood further back, eyes fixed on the floor.

Ned ignored the hum of shock in the sanctuary as parents learned Mrs. Collins' name. Instead, he crouched to Ellie's level, giving her a warm smile. "God doesn't measure worth by the color of our skin, kiddo. And if He made you to look like Miss Caroline one day, that'd be pretty awesome, indeed."

Ellie beamed, patting Caroline's cheek like that settled everything.

Caroline blinked fast, chin high, as she picked Ellie up and walked her to the back where the kids were devouring all the Christmas cookies.

Darcy knew this was the moment that he would always remember about this year's nativity play. He wouldn't recall crooked halos nor the awkward myrrh debate but he would certainly recollect the way truth sounded when someone spoke it without fear and the way Caroline looked like a queen as she stood her ground without flinching.

Later, at Caroline's house, the faint scent of evergreen and sugar cookies lingered in the air. She shut the front door softly, shoulders sagging as silence wrapped around them.

"You okay?" Darcy asked, stepping closer.

She hesitated. "I'm used to it, Darcy. People like Mrs. Collins… they've been around my whole life."

"That doesn't make it right." He caught her hands, threading their fingers together. "Still can't believe her name is Augusta," he murmured.

Caroline let out a low laugh. "Augusta Collins. Sounds like a ship that should've sunk ages ago."

His chuckle rumbled, the tension finally breaking. "You stood tall today. I don't think I've ever been prouder."

Her lips trembled into a soft smile. "You always know what to say."

"Not always." He searched her eyes, wanting her to see his anger still burning on her behalf and the awe she stirred in him. "Sometimes I just know what not to leave unsaid." He drew her closer, one hand sliding to the curve of her waist. "Caroline," he said, voice low and certain, "you are my hero."

She tipped forward, fingers curling into his shirt and he kissed her, pulling her into an embrace that steadied rather than consumed. It was the warmth that came after a winter chill, the surety of arms closing around her when everything else had felt sharp and cold.

When they finally broke apart, she didn't step back but rested her head on his chest, shoulders softening for the first time since the rehearsal.

"We leave it all behind us," he murmured into her hair. "The past, the ghosts... Lizzie. All of it. Don't ever stop believing that you're my future, Caroline. Only you."

A startled laugh slipped out of her, shaky but real. "You mean that?"

"With everything I am," he said simply, "and everything I'll ever be."

Her eyes steadied, her mouth curving into the smallest, most certain smile he'd seen all day. "Okay," she whispered.

CHAPTER 17

Rick

Rick's kids had finally drifted off. Ellie was curled up with her stuffed animals, Lily's bowl of popcorn had slipped from her hand and was now on the floor near the boys who were tangled in their blankets like puppies as the movie credits rolled on the television.

Clicking off the television, Rick pulled out the envelope that had been burning a hole in his shirt pocket since the nativity rehearsal.

Back in March when Darcy had offered Rick Anne Elliot's letter when he was recovering in the hospital, he knew he couldn't bear to read it so he'd asked Darcy to keep it until the time when he was ready to read it. Apparently that was today as Darcy had passed him the envelope at church.

Like ripping off a band-aid, Rick tore open the envelope quick before he could rethink his decision. Anne's careful handwriting stared back at him, heavy and haunting.

Rick,

I have started this letter more times than I can count, and nothing I write feels big enough to hold what I need to say...

I let myself be persuaded by family and by fear that ending our engagement was wise. That you were too much or not enough, depending on who I listened to. And for years I told myself it made sense and I had done you a favor by ending things the way I did... until I learned better didn't.

I would be lying if I did not admit that even after I left California, even after I married Peter and we had children, I wondered where you were, how you were, and if you'd forgiven me.

When I learned the truth about what my twin sister had done... about you being the father of my niece and nephews ... I wept until I couldn't breathe. That you had been there all along, fighting for life while I stood in judgment from afar.

I have asked God's forgiveness a thousand times for not being braver when it mattered most. For not fighting for you. But now I need to ask you for your forgiveness too.

Please forgive me, Rick, for letting other people's doubts and my own tell me you were not worth choosing. I will always be grateful for the part of my life that belonged to you, and I will always hope and pray that you find the happiness you fought harder for than anyone I've ever known.

Be kind to your heart. Be good to yourself. Raise those beautiful children knowing that on behalf of my sister and family, I am so sorry for the way my nieces and nephews' lives had to start. And when you are ready, I pray God will send you someone worthy of all the grace and strength you have shown.

With respect and hope,
Anne

Rick read it three times before he could breathe.

It didn't hurt the way he expected. It felt like a clean break. Like someone had cracked open a window in a locked room. Relief slid through him, strange and heavy, like he was finally free to put down something he hadn't realized he was still carrying.

He thought of that day in the ambulance when Marianne had asked if she should call someone on his behalf and Anne's name had been on the tip of his tongue. But she wasn't his anymore. Maybe she never had been. That door had closed long before Louisa locked him in her deranged world.

He pulled out his phone and scrolled to George's name. His thumb hovered, then tapped.

"Knightley."

"It's Rick. You home?"

"I am. You all right?"

"I will be," Rick said honestly. "Can you sit with the kids for an hour or two?"

"Of course. Give me five minutes."

The ocean wind stung his face, but he barely felt it as he climbed the steps to Marianne's condo. He didn't call first; the letter burned in his pocket like it couldn't wait another second. His knock came harder than he meant.

Footsteps. The deadbolt turned.

"Rick? What's the matter? It's almost eleven."

"I know." His voice came out rough. "I need you to read something."

Elinor, in a fuzzy pink bathrobe, peeked at him from behind Marianne. "Everything okay?"

"No," Rick said simply.

Marianne gave her sister a look. Elinor nodded, retreated to her room and shut the door.

Rick held out the letter. "It's from Anne. I finally read it tonight."

Her voice softened. "And you want me to—"

"Read it. Please. I need you to hear it with me."

She smoothed the paper and began reading aloud. Each word spoken into the quiet room felt like something fragile and holy. When she reached the end, her hand lingered on the page, eyes shimmering.

For a long moment, silence held then her fingers brushed his.

"Thank you for trusting me with that."

"I couldn't imagine sharing it with anyone else," he said honestly.

"You honor me."

He swallowed. "She prayed God would send me someone worthy."

Marianne's hand stilled as she looked up into his eyes.

He looked at this woman who had walked straight into his ruin and never flinched. "I think... Rather, I know that He already has."

Her eyes shimmered with surprise, then something fiercer. "Good," she whispered, voice trembling with emotion. "If she'd wanted you back, I'd have fought her for you and the kids. And I like to think I'd win."

A laugh that sounded a lot like a choke escaped him. "No contest."

"Good answer." Her eyes dropped to his throat and to the scar that reminded them all of the ten years Louisa had kept him a prisoner chained in the cellar.

Before he could react, she leaned forward and kissed it.

His whole body went taut, breath catching with the old instinct to pull back then softening when he felt the care in Marianne's touch. It was loving and respectful. He exhaled, hand sliding into her hair as he let her lips linger there, allowing someone for the first time to touch what once had been a mark of shame.

When she lifted her head, he kissed her hard, everything spilling into one reckless rush. She gasped and in turn her hands pulled him closer until there was no space between them but heat and heartbeats.

"Rick," she breathed, his name like a vow.

"Marianne," he whispered back, kissing her jaw, the line of her throat, memorizing the soft catch of her breath.

Her hands fisted in his hair and pulled him back to her mouth, fierce and unashamed. The letter crinkled on the table beside them, already forgotten.

When they finally broke apart, her thumb traced the scar again. "We're really doing this, aren't we? Letting go of the past?"

"Yeah," he whispered, brushing his lips against her temple. "I don't want to lose out on what God's given us."

Her answering smile radiated with love.

Letting the moment wash over them, they sat there, knees touching, the letter between them like some fragile bridge. After a spell, Marianne stood and crossed to the small cabinet by the tree, pulling out a tiny white box. "I was saving this for Christmas morning, but…"

Inside was a simple wooden ornament, carved in the shape of a lighthouse with *First Christmas – Rick & Marianne* burned into the base.

His throat closed. "You made this?"

"My dad taught me to wood-burn when I was a kid." She smiled, a little shy. "Thought it could go on the tree as proof we made it through our first Christmas together."

Rick swallowed hard, words failed him so he kissed her slowly with gratitude and hope.

When they pulled back, he pressed his forehead to hers, breath uneven. "Thank you."

"Don't thank me," she whispered. "Just... hang it on the tree tomorrow and remember I love you."

Relief slid through him like warm light after years of cold. He tucked her close, the ornament still warm in his hand, and knew some doors hadn't closed on him but rather opened to better rooms than he ever could have imagined.

CHAPTER 18

Darcy

The sanctuary still hummed with leftover chatter from the morning service, sunlight spilling through stained glass onto polished wood. Pine garlands draped the railings, their scent mingling with coffee and pastry crumbs from fellowship hour. Instead of dispersing for lunch, half of Croft Beach had stayed for the children's Nativity play, directed (or more accurately, wrangled) by Lucy Ferrars. Parents and grandparents filled the pews, phones and cameras poised like they were covering a red-carpet premiere.

Darcy sat with Caroline, Rick, and Marianne in a front pew. Caroline's hand rested lightly on his knee, her thumb tracing back and forth, an unconscious rhythm that stirred something in his heart.

The lights dimmed slightly as Lucy stepped to the podium, clutching her clipboard like a life raft, as she ushered her enthusiastic cast into position. Ellie's crooked halo bobbed as she whispered her lines to herself with solemnity. Lily hovered by the other kids playing innkeepers while Sam and Walter peeked around the cardboard stable, bickering before stomping dramatically offstage. A ripple of laughter swept through the pews watching the Wise Men exit stage left as Lucy lifted the microphone.

"Thank you for staying after service," she said brightly despite the way her eyes flickered over to the door where the boys had vanished through. "These kids have worked hard to share the greatest story ever told."

The pianist struck up *O Little Town of Bethlehem*. Caroline leaned into Darcy's shoulder as they listened to the off-key singers, and for one crazy moment, it felt like a dozen Christmases wrapped up in one.

After the song, the light picked up on Maria sitting on a stool in her blue robe. Ellie marched up, hands on her hips, halo crooked. "Don't be 'fraid," she announced, voice ringing clear to the back pew. Maria giggled, throwing her off-script, and Ellie stage-whispered to Lucy, "Is it Jesus or Baby God?"

The sanctuary erupted. Maria covered her face; Lucy ducked behind her clipboard; someone in the choir snorted. "Just... Jesus," Lucy prompted.

Ellie nodded solemnly. "You will have a baby and name Him Jesus." She hugged Maria so fiercely it nearly knocked the halo off, then pranced back to the angel bench, grinning like she'd just saved Christmas.

After another couple songs and scenes, the shepherds shuffled forward with Ava Collins among them, fidgeting behind a cardboard sheep. Ellie leapt up again, wings flapping. "Don't be 'fraid! Glory to God!"

"Is she done yet?" Ava Collins muttered, loud enough for half the sanctuary to hear.

Ellie stomped to her, wings quivering. "No! Shush up and listen! Jesus is born. You need to go see Him about your sins."

Silence.

Ava flushed crimson and glanced at her mother as Ellie nodded firmly. "I'm done now."

Lucy cleared her throat, valiantly hiding a grin. "Thank you, angels and shepherds. Now, we have Mary and Joseph's journey to Bethlehem..."

Maria and a reluctant Johnny Jennings, playing Joseph, solemnly walked up the aisle as the angel choir began another song. As if in slow motion, Johnny stuck out his tongue at his mother along the way causing Rick to lean toward Darcy. "At least it's not just my kids," he muttered. Darcy nearly lost it as he saw Priscilla Jennings try to leap out from her seat only for her husband to hold her down as he started chuckling.

As the pianist sat back, the first innkeeper shook their head at Johnny and Maria saying, "no room." Johnny's older sister as the second innkeeper did the same. Then the third knock. Lily stepped up, holding a bold **NO ROOM** sign and before anyone could say anything she flipped it over. On the back, in uneven bright letters, she had written **JESUS MAKES ROOM FOR EVERYBODY**.

The sanctuary stilled. Lily's voice rang out, strong and certain: "I have no room in the inn but you can have the stable because God says everyone belongs."

Rick froze beside Darcy, eyes bright. Darcy understood why. Last Christmas, Lily had been chained in a cellar by her own mother. Now she was declaring before their entire town that *everyone* belonged. Caroline's hand tightened on his. He hoped she had heard it too because *she* belonged here and wherever she wanted to be.

Back on stage, Lucy blinked fast and cleared her throat. "Thank you, Mary, Joseph and Innkeepers. And now…if the wise men are ready we have the presenting of the gifts."

On cue, Sam and Walter pushed open the sanctuary doors and marched proudly down the aisle hauling a pink wooden doll bed between them. The audience and children alike seemed to freeze in confusion.

Sam puffed up his chest. "We have come from the East to bring gifts for baby Jesus."

Walter nodded seriously. "And a proper bed. Uncle Darcy said He wasn't in a manger when the wise men got there. He was in a house. Right, Uncle Darcy?"

Dozens of heads turned toward Darcy. Caroline buried her face in his shoulder, shaking with laughter. With all eyes on him, Darcy cleared his throat. "Technically... yes it was a house."

Walter gestured grandly. "So, we bring Him a real bed."

"It's a lot better than all that silly myrrh stuff," Sam quickly added.

Maria placed the baby doll carefully in the pink bed, politely bewildered, while Lucy soldiered on, clipboard pressed to her mouth. For one shining, chaotic moment, the whole room rose to sing *Away in a Manger* as the children gathered around that pink bed.

It was not the most clean-cut version of the nativity to be performed but Darcy felt something shift deep in his chest. This little play, messy and unexpected, had said out loud what his heart hadn't been able to communicate. There *was* room for them all. For Caroline. For the kids. For him. For the life they were building. God's plan was louder, braver, and more whole than anyone could ever imagine.

For the first time all week, Darcy believed Croft Beach might actually be big enough for all of them.

CHAPTER 19
Rick

Once the applause faded and the last "Merry Christmas!" echoed through the sanctuary, it took twenty minutes for Rick and the crew to help corral the kids, help put away the props—including the now infamous pink doll bed—and make it to the parking lot.

Ellie had refused to remove her tinsel halo, clutching it in one fist like treasure. "It's for keeps," she announced, already planning to wear it at least through New Year's. Tugging on his hand as the family hurried to the SUV, Ellie buzzed with post-performance adrenaline, cheeks flushed and words tumbling out faster than he could keep up.

"Daddy, I told Maria she can hold my penguin for the next play, and then we should do a princess play, and I can be Elsa and an angel at the same time—"

He caught maybe one word in three, but it didn't matter. Rick crouched and wrapped his arms around her, pressing a kiss to her temple and breathing in the warm, familiar scent of crayons and sugar cookies. For a moment he just held her, listening to the sound of her joy. Had he really once feared he'd never hear her sweet voice ever again?

Darcy clapped his shoulder as they reached the cars. "Burgers?"

"Thought you'd never ask."

The diner off Pacific Coast Highway was crowded with other pageant families in Christmas sweaters and Sunday best. They managed to squeeze into a corner booth with Darcy and Caroline on one side, Marianne and Rick on the other, plus George, Lucy,

Eddie, Maria and her mom, Graciela, and all four Wentworth kids taking every spare chair. Within minutes, half the table was sticky with chocolate shakes and ketchup. Sam lobbied Pastor Eddie to make the pink doll bed an official church prop. Ellie demonstrated her "correct" fry-dipping technique ("You swirl, Maria, not dunk—swirl"), while Walter was trying to convince George to come over for Christmas breakfast at the house.

His brave Lily, sat quietly at first, hands wrapped around her root beer float. Then she lifted her chin, cheeks warming. "Can I make a toast?"

The table stilled.

Lily drew a steady breath and raised her glass. "To Christmas," she said clearly. "To having a tree with real lights, and a warm house, and no mean chains on our feet." Lily hesitated, glancing at Caroline. "Just Aunt Caroline's anklet because she had said I deserved something pretty to remind me I'm free."

Caroline's hand flew to her mouth, eyes shining. Rick couldn't trust his voice, so he squeezed Lily's shoulder instead, pride swelling until it hurt.

She met his eyes, full of hope and excitement. "And to everyone here who made this the best Christmas I ever had."

The table was silent except for Ellie's soft slurp of her shake.

Caroline leaned across, cupping Lily's face. "Sweetheart, you have no idea how proud we are of you."

Darcy raised his glass, voice rough. "To belonging. All of us."

They lifted their drinks—root beer, coffee, shakes, water—and clinked them together. The sound was soft and bright, like an amen.

Lunch stretched into the afternoon, long after most families had gone. The kids wilted one by one—Ellie curled up in Rick's lap; Walter was leaning contently against George's shoulder; Sam slouched in a corner of the booth; Lily resting her chin in her hands but smiling as Caroline teased Darcy about his "theological accuracy" comment about the wise men.

For a while, Rick just breathed it in. This loud, sweet, chaotic moment was one he never dreamt he'd see last Christmas. Thanks to God, he and the children were safe, free, and surrounded by people who'd fought for them when they couldn't fight for themselves.

Later, back at the beach house, the kids tumbled toward bed half-asleep and sticky from their chocolate shakes while Marianne and Rick lingered at the door. The halo dangled from Rick's hand, a reminder of the wonder of the day.

"That was some toast," Marianne said softly, eyes warm.

"Yeah." He swallowed, thinking of Lily's steady voice and the anklet glinting on her ankle. "A year ago, I didn't think we'd ever have this. I wasn't even sure I would ever see Walter, Sam, and Ellie again in this lifetime."

Marianne touched his sleeve, fingers curling gently. "You did it, Rick. You fought for this life."

He shook his head, voice rough. "We fought for it."

For a moment, neither moved. Then she rose on her toes and kissed him slowly, her arms circling his neck as if she had no plans to let go.

Rick's free hand slipped behind her back, pulling her flush against him as the halo clattered softly to the floor.

"Merry Christmas, Marianne," he whispered against her mouth.

She smiled, breath warm on his cheek. "Merry Christmas, Rick."

And he kissed her again, deeper this time, holding her like home had finally found him too.

CHAPTER 20

Darcy

Croft Beach's boardwalk hummed with holiday energy. Families were darting into decorated shopfronts in search of last-minute gifts, white lights spiraled up lampposts, and evergreen wreaths glowed in every doorway. Caroline's hand was warm in Darcy's, her laughter soft and unguarded as they strolled past the boutiques.

"Did you know about Lily's sign that she created for the nativity?" Caroline shook her head, smiling in remembrance. "That girl's smarter than half the adults I know."

"She gets it from her dad," Darcy said.

Caroline's fingers squeezed his. "I love days like this when it feels like Heaven on earth."

The words landed deep but he was still unprepared when she added softly, "Do you ever think it'd be easier somewhere else?"

He stopped walking abruptly to turn and face her. "If you ever want to leave—if this place won't let you breathe—say the word."

Her eyes softened. "And you'd really go?"

"I'd pack the car tonight."

She brushed her thumb across his knuckles. "I don't know if I want to run. I'm just tired fighting for my place here."

"You shouldn't have to fight at all," he said quietly.

A faint smile touched her lips. "I have a feeling things are going to only get more interesting. Your Aunt Catherine and your cousin William are flying in tonight and my cousin Tabitha is flying in tomorrow. I hope your Aunt Catherine doesn't scare her off in five minutes."

"My aunt? Your cousin?" He grinned. "If she's your cousin, I'm sure she'll handle Aunt Catherine just fine. And I'm looking forward to meeting her and her husband, Jordan."

Caroline laughed but quieter now, like she was bracing for something unnamed.

At Newport Palms Hotel, Darcy's sister Georgie stood by the doors with one small purse waiting for him. No suitcase was in sight. She didn't smile. Caroline's hand tightened slightly on his as he pulled the car to a halt outside the entrance.

"Is Lizzie still in town?" Darcy asked as Georgie climbed into the backseat.

"She is in our room," Georgie said quickly. "She didn't want another scene but you should know that she's as welcome in Croft Beach as Caroline is, if not more."

Caroline's fingers slipped into her coat pocket. It was an old habit Darcy recognized as a defense mechanism.

"We've been over this," he said quietly.

"She's alone on Christmas," Georgie's voice thinned. "She doesn't have anybody, Darcy."

"She has family. Options. And we are not her family." His tone sharpened.

Georgie's eyes flashed, then faltered when she glanced forward at Caroline sitting quietly in the front passenger seat.

"You've changed," she muttered.

"Yes," Darcy said evenly as he pulled onto the freeway. "And I'm not sorry."

Aunt Catherine waited for them just past luggage claim at the airport, posture razor-straight, gloved hands folded like she'd never touched anything ordinary in her life.

"William," she called coolly, barely glancing at her son pushing the luggage cart before turning her trademark measured gaze on her nephew. After a minute, her eyes slid past him, landing on Caroline with surgical precision.

"These situations are always… complicated." Her tone sharpened. "Some people thrive in them provided they don't mind trading their reputation for attention. Let's only hope this Christmas spectacle and upcoming wedding don't tarnish our family's good name in the community."

It landed like a slap. Caroline flinched, color draining from her face, her hands curling into tight fists at her sides.

Darcy's blood went hot. "Caroline isn't a *spectacle*," he said, voice sharp enough to turn heads. "She's the woman I'm going to marry and you'd best remember that, Aunt Catherine, or you won't be welcome in my house."

Aunt Catherine's mouth pinched into an elegant, disapproving line, but she said nothing more. Cousin William mouthed *sorry* and Georgie stared back at him hard, unrepentant.

By the time he turned around, Caroline was already striding toward the exit, shoulders tight, pace clipped.

"Caroline!" He shoved past a knot of travelers and jogged after her, catching up just as she pushed through the doors into the cold.

She stopped but didn't turn, her breath clouding white in the winter air.

He caught her hand. "Don't let her steal this from us. We were so happy this afternoon."

Hurt flickered behind the steel in her eyes as she finally looked at him. She let him lace his fingers through hers, holding on for a long, silent beat before kissing his cheek and turning back toward the taxi queue.

CHAPTER 21

Rick

Rick had just settled the kids in the den with mugs of cocoa when his phone buzzed.

Darcy: You home?

Rick: Yeah. What's up?

Darcy: Mind if I come over? Need you.

Which, translated knowing Darcy, Rick translated to mean he was hanging on by a thread.

Ten minutes later, Darcy stepped through the sliding door like he'd walked off a battlefield—hair mussed, shoulders tight, no small talk. He braced both hands on the kitchen counter and bowed his head. Rick gave him a beat, then popped the lid off a beer and slid it across.

Darcy huffed something like a laugh, but it didn't stick.

"Bad, huh?" Rick asked.

"You have no idea." Darcy drained half the bottle in one swallow.

"Aunt Catherine hasn't changed. She is as judgmental as ever before with a tongue sharp enough to cut steel. My cousin William tried to referee, but even he couldn't keep up. And Georgie…" His voice faltered, rough now. "She just stood there. My own sister didn't defend Caroline. Didn't say a word."

He rubbed a hand over his face. "Caroline walked out. She took a freaking taxi, Rick! She texted me that she'd see me later and that was it." He stared at the countertop like it might give him answers. "Christmas Eve is in three days and our wedding in ten days and I never felt so powerless.."

Rick stayed quiet, letting him fill the silence.

"Aunt asked if I realized the so-called 'scrutiny' I was inviting, and whether she had to accept our relationship. Darn her! She actually called Caroline a spectacle like she was some holiday stunt. I told them Caroline isn't a spectacle and that she's the woman I'm going to marry. I meant it. Every word." His voice cracked. "But Caroline still walked out. And right now... it feels like I might've lost her."

Rick leaned against the counter, his hand held out in support. "You didn't lose her, Darcy. You hit a wall called Catherine de Borough. It's a big difference."

"It doesn't feel different," Darcy muttered.

"That's because you care," Rick said simply. "If you didn't, you'd shrug it off and go to bed."

Darcy shook his head. "She's been so patient through all of this. Tonight though felt like a test that I failed."

"Not a test," Rick said. "It's just a moment that showed you both where things stand. You can fix that. Darcy, you just have to show up. Caroline doesn't need you to win every family argument. What she needs is for you to show her that you won't let go of her hand when it gets ugly."

Darcy stared at the floor for a long beat, then nodded. "You think she'll forgive me for letting her walk away?"

"Darcy, she called a taxi, not a moving van. She went home to breathe, not to leave you. But you need to tell her how you feel and the sooner the better. You don't want to wait for her to guess, and add two and two and make five."

Darcy exhaled, some of the tightness in his shoulders finally easing. "Thanks," he murmured.

"Anytime," Rick said. "You did the same for me when I couldn't breathe on my own after my rescue."

Darcy's mouth twitched, almost a smile. "I should go. Try to head this off before it festers."

"Good plan," Rick agreed, as he opened the front door. "And Darcy—"

He looked back.

"You're not failing. You're fighting. Don't forget the difference."

For once, Darcy didn't argue.

Rick lingered on the porch after Darcy left, the moon silvering the waves and cool air stinging his lungs. He didn't hear his phone ring in his pocket but immediately called Marianne back as he got comfortable on the stoop.

"Darcy all right?" she asked softly as soon as he'd explained the situation.

"He will be. Just family stuff—ugly and complicated. I told him to go talk to Caroline and not let things go unsaid."

"Rick, speaking of not letting things go unsaid… can I ask you something? And I need you to be honest."

"Always."

Her voice was barely above a whisper. "When Pastors Ned and Fanny came over to Darcy's… You know how I said I sometimes don't feel enough for you? I can't stop thinking about that moment. About Louisa. About how much she… took from you."

His chest tightened. "Marianne—"

"I know you said you never felt love for the witch, and I believe you. But sometimes I wonder if I can ever measure up. If, when we're married, you'll expect things I can't give you. What if I'm not able to please you? Or you're comparing me to Louisa every time we're together?"

He longed to look her in the face as he tried to reassure her. "Hey. Listen at me. She didn't teach me love, Marianne. Everything she took from me was against my will. What I felt with her was fear and a need for survival, not passion and trust. Know what I feel with you? I feel choice, freedom, love, peace, and hope. I'm not comparing you to her because there's no comparison. She took; you give. She caged me; you set me free."

Her voice sounded choked with tears as she replied. "You have no idea how much I needed to hear that."

"Please don't ever forget that, Marianne Dashwood. You're enough for me. More than enough. And when it's our wedding night, it's going to be about us. We'll leave all the exes and nightmares behind. No ghosts and no expectations. Just you and me choosing each other, okay?"

"I love you, Rick Wentworth."

"I love you too," he said softly. "No more ghosts," he whispered. "Not between us."

Marianne's voice was steady now as smile sighed. "I'm holding you to that, Mr. Wentworth."

CHAPTER 22

Darcy

The restaurant smelled of garlic and roasting vegetables, warm and inviting against the December chill. Darcy had chosen it carefully for their last date night before the Christmas festivities. It was undoubtedly Caroline's favorite restaurant and the atmosphere quiet enough after the pageant weekend to feel like it belonged to just them. He'd even planned a beach walk and harbor lights boat ride afterward.

They hadn't even sat down however before a voice cut through the room.

"Fitz?"

Only one person called him by his first name. Aunt Catherine. Her voice rang out crisp and commanding making it impossible to ignore.

They turned to see her at a corner table with Georgie, Lizzie Bennet, and William. Georgie's shoulders hunched like she wanted to disappear and William offered a faint, strained smile.

"Hello, everyone." Darcy schooled his features. "I didn't expect to see you tonight."

"Obviously not." Catherine's gaze slid to Caroline, expression pinched and cool. "You were invited but Georgie said you were busy. I could have forgiven you working on an important case or knee deep in wedding plans even but this? A date over your family? Need I remind you that I'm your only aunt? Perhaps these days family means something different to you, my boy."

He bristled at being called a boy and was about to say something when Caroline's hand grasped his. "Good evening, Aunt Catherine," she said evenly.

"I'm not your aunt, young lady."

Despite Darcy's grip on her hand, Caroline held her ground. "I used to think if I stayed quiet, maybe I'd deserve a seat at tables like this. But I finally realized the table isn't yours to give."

For a moment, Catherine blinked, startled, before recovering her icy calm. "How quaint. I only hope you know what you're doing, Fitz," she said, deliberately using his given name like a weapon. "Your... choices have a way of attracting attention and not the good kind. I'd hate for this Christmas spectacle and your upcoming wedding to leave a stain that's hard to remove."

William shifted uncomfortably. "Mom, can we not do this here?"

Grateful to his cousin, Darcy gave him a brief nod but that gratitude faded as he saw his own sister look away.

"How many times do I have to tell you, Aunt Catherine, that Caroline isn't a spectacle," Darcy bit out. "She's the woman I'm going to marry and if you can't accept that, perhaps you'd better go back home."

His aunt's eyebrows rose. "We'll see how long your bravado lasts." She stood, gathering her coat like armor. "Fitz, do try to remember you are a Darcy of Croft Beach. If nothing else, think what you're doing to poor Georgiana and her reputation in this town."

With those parting words, she swept out, the door jingling shut behind her.

For a moment, no one breathed. A couple of diners glanced their way before quickly looking away.

Georgie stood, chewing her lip. "Darcy, I just want to see you happy."

He met his sister's eyes. "Then support my relationship with Caroline. That's all I'm asking."

Georgie flushed, nodded once, and mumbled, "Okay."

Lizzie offered a faint, awkward, "good to see you," before following her out with William.

Darcy guided Caroline to their table, covering her hand with his. "I'm sorry for the way she spoke to you," he whispered.

She gave a shaky laugh. "She's never going to change."

Dinner itself was quiet with Caroline picking at her pasta as Darcy tried to keep the conversation light. By dessert, some color had returned to her cheeks.

When they stepped outside, he took her hand. "Come with me. I've got one more thing planned."

Curiosity flickered in her eyes. "Something else?"

"Trust me."

The December air was brisk, the ocean restless under a scattering of stars. He led her down the boardwalk to a small private dock, where a yacht decked out in Christmas lights waited.

And standing on it, grinning and waving, were her cousin Tabitha and her husband, Jordan.

Caroline froze, her free hand flying to her mouth. "You didn't."

"I did," Darcy said softly. "I wanted you to have a night surrounded by love. Not scrutiny. Not judgment. Just love."

Tabitha hopped lightly onto the dock and hugged Caroline tight. "Girl, you didn't tell me Croft Beach drama was this spicy," she teased.

Caroline laughed, the sound breaking free like she'd been holding it in for hours. "You came all the way out here just for this?"

"We came for *you*," Tabitha said firmly. "And how could we turn down a ride in style on this yacht?!"

They climbed aboard, the lights reflecting on the harbor like a thousand tiny stars. Caroline stayed close as the boat pulled away from the dock.

"You really planned all this?" she whispered.

"I wanted you to know," he murmured against her hair, "that you are loved. By me. By them."

Her eyes closed, lashes damp, but she smiled. "You're ridiculous," she said softly. "We already saw these lights."

"But not like this. Last time some people tried to ruin it for you."

Tabitha grinned from the bow where she was sipping champagne. "He definitely gets my vote of approval."

Jordan chuckled. "Very smooth. I'll give him that."

Caroline laughed again, tension finally breaking. She pulled back to look at him, eyes steady and warm. "I'm glad we stayed, Darcy. Despite all the ugliness tonight… this is what I'm choosing. I choose you and our life together no matter where we are."

Before he could respond, she curled her fingers in his lapel, pulled him down, and kissed him unapologetically as if she was declaring to the world that she was the proud future Mrs. Darcy.

When she finally drew back, her lips curved in a smile that made his heart stutter. "That's my answer to every table, every room, every person who thinks I don't belong at your side," she declared. "I'm not leaving. I'm done with hiding. And I'm definitely not giving you up."

He slid his hand over hers on the railing, thumb brushing her engagement ring. The emerald he'd chosen because it reminded him of her heritage, her roots, and her strength gleamed back at them. Around them, the yacht's crew moved quietly, passing out petit fours and more chilled champagne as the lights from the harbor rippled across the water.

Together, they watched the reflections shimmer like a private constellation, hand in hand, until the drama from earlier seemed to have been driven away.

CHAPTER 23

Rick

Rick had never done this with his kids. Not once.

Some naïve part of him had imagined Louisa gave them magical Christmases upstairs while he and Lily were locked in the basement. Surely there had been Santa visits, messy cookie baking episodes, and crooked stars hanging from the Christmas trees. But as they walked toward the Santa hut on the Croft Beach boardwalk, he learned how wrong he'd been.

Sam trudged ahead, hands deep in his coat pockets. "Mom never let us see Santa. Said it was too... what's the word?"

Walter scowled. "Commercialized."

Lily's voice came soft, too soft. "One time, I asked if I could have a Christmas present." Her fingers tightened around Ellie's tiny hand in remembrance. "She slapped me and said I should be lucky she let me live."

Rick's chest constricted. Caroline blinked fast and slid an arm around Lily's trembling shoulders. Her cousin Tabitha likewise rested a hand gently on Lily's back.

Ellie, blissfully unaware of the heaviness, skipped toward the glowing Santa hut. "But this time we get to do Santa, right, Daddy?"

Rick squeezed her hand, forcing a smile as he gently corrected her grammar. "This time we get to see Santa. Yes, Little Love."

The Santa hut looked like something from a snow globe. There was candy-cane trim, plastic icicles, and a leaning North Pole sign jammed into the sand. Inside, it smelled like cinnamon and hot cocoa.

Santa's beard was a little crooked, but his eyes were kind. "Ho, ho, ho! Who do we have here?"

Ellie darted forward and immediately spilled every thought in her head. "Hi! I'm Ellie, I'm three, and I have a penguin named Flippers and a duck named Quackers, and I've been mostly good except when Walter takes my crayons and makes me cry. Can I have more duckies so Quackers isn't lonely?"

Walter groaned. "Ellie..."

Santa winked. "We'll see what we can do, young lady."

Sam asked for a new soccer ball, Walter wanted a new fishing pole, and then it was Lily's turn.

Santa's voice softened as she climbed onto the bench. "And what would you like for Christmas, young lady?"

Lily's chin trembled, but she sat straighter, clutching the cushion edge. "I know you couldn't visit me when I was chained in the cellar," she said seriously, her earnest voice carrying through the hush that fell over the crowd. "But I'm free now, Santa. And I was hoping you could come visit us this year. We have a chimney and stockings, and it's not as scary as the cellar was. You'll be safe."

She turned, looking at Rick, solemn and brave. "Daddy told me why you couldn't visit. But you would be safe this year. Right, Daddy?"

Rick's throat locked as he nodded. "That's right, baby. It is safe now."

Santa's gloved hands curled gently over hers. "Thank you for the invitation, Lily. I would be honored to visit your house."

She nodded firmly. "Okay. And... if it's not too much trouble, I'd like a dog. His name's Daniel. Like in the lions' den. So he can protect us. And he can be mine. No one can take him away."

Santa's eyes glistened behind his glasses. "That's a very special wish. Daniel will be lucky to have you."

Rick froze. That voice was deep, warm, and familiar. He almost said the name of his old high school history teacher, Mr. Peters, but caught himself just in time. Lily was still chattering about the joy of Christmas, blissfully unaware. Santa winked at him, like he knew the near-slip had happened.

Santa chuckled as Lily gave him a big hug before jumping off the bench then he looked at Rick, eyes bright with something unspoken. "And what about you, Dad? What do you want for Christmas?"

The question caught him off guard. He glanced at his kids and sighed.

"Honestly?" His voice came out rough. "I've already got it. A safe home. My kids laughing again. People who don't give up on us. That's more than I thought I'd ever have."

Santa leaned closer, voice low. "That's a good list, Dad. But I've got a feeling you've got one more wish in you somewhere."

Rick rubbed the back of his neck, chuckling. "I don't think so, Santa. I'm good. I've got everything I need right here."

Curiously he turned and followed Santa's lion of sight as his eyes flicked past him to the jewelry store across the boardwalk. In its window, a ring shimmered under a spotlight, catching every Christmas light strung along the street. Rick would be lying if he denied that he'd eyed it a few times himself.

Santa smiled knowingly and murmured, "Mm-hmm. Looks like you just thought of it."

Heat crept up Rick's neck. "That obvious, huh?"

Santa chuckled, patting his shoulder. "Go take a look."

"Daddy, what's Santa talking about?" Ellie piped up. "Are we getting more ducks?"

Walter snorted. "Bet it's socks."

Rick shook his head, grinning. "Santa and I just had a grown-up talk."

Santa winked. "Merry Christmas, Rick."

"Merry Christmas, Santa."

Rick left the kids with Caroline and Tabitha, bribed with candy canes and cocoa, and crossed to the jewelry store.

The ring was even more beautiful up close. It was simple and elegant just like Marianne herself.

Inside, the clerk approached, smiling. But before she could speak, a warm voice came from behind him:

"Good taste, Rick. Marianne's a lucky woman."

Rick turned. Santa, still in full costume, stood there, eyes crinkled with that same kindness he'd recognized earlier.

"Mr. Pe—" Rick caught himself, lowering his voice. "Santa…"

A soft chuckle came from under the beard. "Bill, put this one on my tab," he said to the shop owner who had stepped out of his office to greet them.

Rick shook his head. "I can't let you—"

The owner slid the velvet box into Rick's hand with a quiet smile. "Merry Christmas, Rick. From all of us who know what you've been through."

Santa winked again, voice low so only Rick could hear. "Some gifts you don't question, son."

Rick swallowed hard, emotion catching in his throat as he mouthed a bewildered thank you just as the bell jingled and in rushed the kids followed by an amused Caroline and Tabitha. Ellie spotted the little box immediately and gasped. "Daddy, is that for Miss Marianne?"

Walter groaned. "Ellie, you weren't supposed to say anything!"

Sam shrugged. "I mean, it's kind of obvious."

Lily just smiled, soft and proud, like she knew a secret worth keeping.

Rick tucked the box into his pocket and grinned down at them. "One thing at a time, guys."

But as they stepped back onto the boardwalk, his hand holding Ellie's, Rick couldn't help the big grin as Caroline nudged him with a knowing wink.

CHAPTER 24

Darcy

Caroline's holiday playlist drifted through the kitchen speaker. There was everything you could hope for from Ella Fitzgerald, to at least three versions of *Mary, Did You Know?*, and of course Michael Crawford's Christmas album that Darcy had bought for Caroline last year. With the music swirling around the crew working on dinner preparations in the kitchen, Darcy was convinced it couldn't have felt more perfect.

The counters were crowded with flour-dusted cookbooks, cooling trays, and Ellie's lopsided gingerbread house, which she had proudly declared "perfect" before devouring all the gumdrops meant for the roof.

Caroline moved like she owned the space, with her sleeves rolled up, apron dusted with sugar, and her braids threaded with tiny gold beads for the holidays that shimmered when she leaned over Ellie, offering a homemade puff puff.

"I'm gonna eat five," Ellie whispered solemnly.

"Save room for green beans," Caroline teased.

"I'll eat all the green stuff if I can have more after," Ellie bargained, eyes wide with hope.

At the stove Lucy stirred jollof rice nervously. "This is my third time making it. Still can't get it like yours."

"Tonight, it's perfect," Caroline assured her.

Darcy decided to make his presence known as he stepped into the room and leaned across Ellie to steal a puff puff. "You've made this place smell like Christmas."

Caroline looked up and something in her face softened the way it always did when she saw him. It was as if for a moment the rest of the room faded and it was just the two of them in the room. "That was the plan."

The doorbell rang keeping him from getting sappy as he went to let in the first of their guests. Rick ushered in Sam and Walter, both in matching Christmas sweaters, Lily shyly clutching a gift bag, and Elinor trailing politely behind.

"Wow," Elinor murmured, glancing around. "This looks... incredible."

"It's all Caroline," Darcy said, pride thick in his chest.

Caroline, with Ellie perched on her hip, smiled as she stepped into the hall to greet their guests. "Come in. Shoes off. Ellie has declared this a shoe free party."

Sam whooped as he removed his shoes. "Check out my Christmas socks!"

As the kids barreled toward the living room, leaving laughter in their wake, Rick lingered long enough to meet Caroline's eyes. "You always make this house feel like a home," he said quietly.

She ducked her head, smiling. "Thank you, Rick."

For a heartbeat, the room held still. Then Ellie broke it with an eager, "Aunt Caroline? Can I have another puff puff?"

"After dinner." Caroline laughed as she turned back to the kitchen with Ellie to finish the preparations.

With Rick and Elinor's assistance, Darcy finished the final touches in the dining room making the house glow warm and golden in no time before the next guests arrived.

Just as dinner was ready, Aunt Catherine swept in like a cold front, Georgie and William trailing behind her.

"Darcy," William muttered during their handshake, "if this turns into a public referendum on your love life, I'm going back to the hotel."

Darcy smirked faintly. "Can't promise anything."

Without greeting the other guests who were already seated around the table, Aunt Catherine surveyed the buffet like it was a crime scene. Georgie shrank toward a seat next to Lucy, avoiding eye contact with any of the other guests. Caroline who was sitting at the far end of the table beside her cousin, gave Darcy a small, steady nod as if bracing herself for whatever was to come.

Then the doorbell rang again and before anyone could say anything, Darcy's sister rushed out to the hall to answer the door.

Georgie reappeared moments later, smiling like nothing was wrong, with Lizzie Bennet Wickham at her side.

"Merry Christmas, everyone," Lizzie said brightly. "Hope I'm not too late."

The air seemed to have been sucked out of the room. Darcy heard Caroline's soft intake of breath and felt the back of his neck prickle.

He turned to Georgie, voice low. "Are you out of your mind?"

"She was alone," Georgie defended, shifting uncomfortably. "It's Christmas Eve."

"This isn't your call—"

Ellie's small voice floated over the strain in the room. "Uncle Darcy? Can we eat now?"

Caroline looked at him, shoulders tight but face calm. "I'll get another place setting if someone could find an extra seat," she said softly. She rose with grace, Ellie clinging to her neck, and Darcy proudly watched her walk away with dignity in every step.

When she returned to the dining room where everyone was now seated, she gave Pastor Ned a nod. "Would you pray for us?"

Ned's voice carried steady and warm: "Lord, thank You for this table and every person gathered here. Thank You for grace that meets us where we are and love that covers more than we deserve. Bless this meal and those who prepared it. And teach us, especially tonight, how to see one another through Your eyes. Amen."

Spoons clattered as dishes were passed down the table as people pretended nothing had happened to disturb the peaceful atmosphere. But then Catherine spoke.

"I suppose you imagine you've finally arrived sitting at the place of honor," she addressed Caroline coolly from her place at Darcy's right hand side. "But let's be clear that you are here by Fitz's indulgence, not merit of your own. Bastards like these," she gestured dramatically toward Ellie whom Caroline was helping serve a heaping portion of green beans, "cling to any woman who offers them a little sweetness. It doesn't make you their mother. And it doesn't change who you are."

Rick stood, chair legs scraping, fists curled. "You better watch yourself—"

Darcy's own pulse spiked, hot and fast.

"Rick," he said sharply, standing. "This is my fight."

Rick's jaw flexed, but he reluctantly sat back down.

Darcy's voice cut through the room, steady and loud enough to carry. "Aunt Catherine, you don't get to talk about the woman I love like she's an inconvenience. You don't get to dismiss her kindness, her culture, or her place in this home. And you certainly don't get to pretend you're the judge of what a family looks like or use that kind of language to describe Rick's children at my table."

Catherine stiffened. "The Darcys built this town's reputation. It's my duty to protect it from... complications—"

"No." Darcy's throat burned, but his voice only grew stronger. "Caroline has more grace in her smallest kindness than this table has shown all night. She has shown love to everyone here, including me when I didn't deserve it. She belongs exactly where she is. And I—" His voice cracked, but he let it. "I love her. I love how she threads gold beads into her braids because it reminds her of her mother. I love how she holds Ellie like she's her flesh and blood, not just an honorary aunt. And I love how she chooses kindness, even when it costs her."

"What did she call me, Aunt Caroline?" Ellie piped up, looking upset and confused.

A tear slid down Caroline's cheek as she pulled Ellie close into her arms and breathed in her baby powder scent.

Aunt Catherine stood, her chest heaving. "You'll regret this," she snapped, sweeping toward the door.

Georgie hesitated, guilt written plainly on her face, before she turned to Lizzie and they both stood to leave. At the doorway, however, Lizzie lingered, looking at the silent group still sitting at the dining table. For the first time since she'd arrived so unexpectedly in town, her confident posture faltered. Her eyes swept over Darcy as if searching for the charismatic younger man she had known and loved once upon a time.

"Darcy…" Lizzie's voice was softer now, uncertain. "You really love her, don't you?"

Walking over to Caroline's seat, Darcy put his arm around Caroline's shoulders instinctively. "With everything I am," he said simply.

Something flickered in Lizzie's expression—regret? wistfulness?—before she nodded. "Then… I guess I came looking for someone who doesn't exist anymore." She gave a tight, almost sad smile. "Merry Christmas, Caroline. I hope Croft Beach treats you better than tonight."

Caroline, startled, managed a quiet, "Merry Christmas."

Lizzie nodded once more, then followed Georgie into the hall, her steps slower than when she'd arrived.

Hearing the front door click closed, Darcy felt Caroline lean into him, steady and warm and finally felt free to breathe again.

Ellie slipped down from Caroline's lap. Glancing up at the one puff puff left on the buffet table, Ellie hesitated before picking it up and then padded over to Caroline and held it out.

"Here," she whispered. "You can have it, Aunt Caroline. You look like you need it more."

Caroline made a soft, broken sound as she crouched and pulled Ellie close.

When no one else was looking, Darcy gently took Caroline's hand and lifted it to his lips, pressing a soft kiss to her knuckles like it were a silent promise. His heart hammered, not from the fight, but from finally daring to say what he'd held back for too long.

Caroline kissed Ellie's hair, voice trembling but sure as she broke the last puff puff in half and handed one half to Ellie. "This is the sweetest thing anyone's done for me all night."

CHAPTER 25

Rick

The kids were finally asleep. That alone felt like a Christmas miracle.

Rick stood in the middle of the garage, surrounded by cardboard boxes, shredded wrapping paper, and three half-assembled bikes that looked like an OSHA violation waiting to happen. One of the pedals had somehow welded itself emotionally to the wrong chain, and a bolt had rolled under the workbench never to be seen again.

The instruction manual might as well have been in Greek. He'd stared at it so long the diagrams blurred into what looked like abstract art.

Finally, he gave up and texted George Knightley:

Do you have a torque wrench I can borrow?

The reply came fast:

On my way.

Ten minutes later, George stepped through the garage door with his toolkit in hand. He took one look at the chaos and muttered, "Good grief. You weren't kidding."

"Don't judge me," Rick said. "They looked simpler in the store. And no, they didn't have any models pre-assembled."

George smirked, already rolling up his sleeves. "You're lucky I like you and the kids."

Getting down to business, George was steady and quiet while Rick was clumsy but determined. There was something therapeutic about it. The two men who had survived their own unique wreckages worked tirelessly side by side putting something new together bolt by bolt.

When their task was accomplished, Rick wiped his hands on a towel and stepped back. Three gleaming bikes stood lined up in the garage next to a small tricycle for Ellie. "They're going to lose their minds tomorrow."

George smiled faintly, eyes soft. "Merry Christmas, Rick."

"Thanks for coming."

"Wouldn't have missed it."

"Hope we'll see you in the morning. You know Walter and the kids would be disappointed if you didn't make an appearance at some point."

George smiled thoughtfully. "We'll see."

After George left, Rick tucked the bikes under a tarp, double-checked the stockings, and collapsed on the couch. The house—thank God—was finally still.

For about three and a half hours.

At 4:07 a.m., socked feet crept across the hardwood.

Rick cracked one eye open. Three pajama-clad shadows hovered near the tree like tiny Christmas commandos. Lily led the charge, flashlight under her chin like a SWAT team member. Walter peeked over her shoulder, already clutching a stocking he wasn't supposed to touch yet. And Ellie, Rick's sleep-resistant elf, was bouncing in her duck slippers as she blinked up at the Christmas tree she had proudly selected.

"Dad?" Lily whispered. "Are you awake?"

"Nope," he muttered. "This is a decoy dad. Real one is asleep upstairs."

Walter snorted, half-choking on his own laugh.

"But it's Christmas," Ellie insisted, as if that canceled the laws of time and space.

Rick pried one eye open. "What time is it?"

They hesitated.

"Four-oh-seven," Walter finally admitted.

Theatrically, Rick groaned and flopped an arm over his face. "And what time did we agree on?"

"Six," they chorused, unrepentant.

"Exactly."

Ellie crawled onto the couch, nose two inches from his. "But we can't sleep anymore."

"Try," Rick said. "Talk. Whisper. Giggle under the covers. But no opening presents. No waking up your brother. And *no*—" He gave Lily a look. "—sneaking into the garage."

Lily raised an eyebrow. "The garage?"

He groaned. "Nice one, Dad," she muttered.

"Pretend you didn't hear that," he said. "And I'll pretend I don't hear the cookie jar in five minutes."

Ellie kissed his cheek. "You're the best Daddy ever."

Walter gave him a solemn thumbs-up—the universal sign for *we're still going to break the rules.*

"See you at 6:01," Lily whispered as they scampered upstairs.

From the hallway came Sam's bleary voice: "Why are people talking… it's not even light out…"

Ellie stage-whispered back, "It's *CHRISTMAS*, Sam!"

Hearing the boys' bedroom door slam shut again, Rick grinned into the couch cushion as he closed his eyes and let silence settle again. A year ago, he'd woken up in chains, wondering if the world had moved on without him. Wondering if his kids were warm, safe, loved.

Now, the only chains in this house were the ones on three new bikes waiting in the garage—bikes his kids would ride to the beach, to the park, and into a future that didn't look like survival but like living.

This—this chaotic, sweet, too-early mess—was everything he'd never known to dream about.

And when he finally drifted back to sleep, Ellie's kiss still warm on his cheek and the smell of cookies in the air, he dreamed of fours kids squealing over their freedom on wheels as morning sunlight glinted off bright new chains.

CHAPTER 26

Darcy

It was still dark when Darcy rang Caroline's doorbell.

Not just dim but pitch dark, the kind of deep winter pre-dawn where even the Pacific Ocean seemed to be holding its breath. Streetlamps carved out soft halos on the sidewalk, and somewhere far out on the water, a buoy bell rang faintly.

Finally his persistent ringing of the bell paid off as Caroline stood in the doorway barefoot in flannel pajama pants and a robe, her braids tied back for sleep. Tabitha peeked over her shoulder as Jordan calling from deeper in the house, "Everything okay?"

Darcy stepped back, almost ashamed of the urgency that had dragged him here before dawn.

"I didn't mean to wake everyone," he apologized to the group at large as he looked at Caroline with a plea in his eyes.

After deliberating for a moment, Caroline looked over her shoulder, gave Tabitha a little nod, then stepped out onto the porch, struggling into a jacket and pair of boots.

"Can we walk?" he asked.

They walked in silence down to the beach. The tide whispered, the air cool enough to sting. He stopped near the waterline, his breath misting like smoke.

Caroline stopped just short of the dunes, arms wrapped tight against the chill. "Your house was one place that was supposed to be safe. And you knew—." Her voice caught, low but steady as she reigned in her feelings. "You knew your aunt thinks I don't belong. You knew Lizzie wasn't there for Christmas cheer. And I sat there alone, feeling like I'd been fed to the lions with only Ellie as my ally. Do you know how that feels?"

Darcy didn't flinch, didn't look away. "You're right. I didn't want to make things worse with Georgie so I let Lizzie stay and instead I made things worse for you." His jaw tightened, regret threading every word. "I let them make you feel small in a place where you should have only felt wanted and safe."

Her arms loosened slightly, eyes glistening. "It was the first time your home didn't feel like *ours*, Darcy."

He stepped closer, voice rough. "That's on me. I should have protected that space for you. I should have made it crystal clear from the start that you're not just welcome but that you *belong*. And I swear to you, Caroline, that no one gets to question that again. Not Aunt Catherine. Not Lizzie. Not even Georgie."

Caroline stared at him, hurt and love warring in her expression. "Words are easy, Darcy."

"I know." His hands gently cupped her face, steady but soft. "I'll prove it not with flowers or rings or big speeches, but by choosing you every single time, even when it's uncomfortable just like I chose you over my Aunt Catherine. In fact, I booked a seat on the morning flight back home for Aunt Catherine and William has agreed to put her in a taxi in the morning. Please hear me. I chose you, Caroline Bingley."

For a long beat, she just looked at him searching for hesitation and finding none. Finally, she exhaled, tension slipping from her shoulders. "Good," she whispered, voice shaking but sure. "Because I'm not walking into another lions' den alone."

172

His forehead lowered to hers. "Never again," he promised, then kissed her like he meant every word.

By the time they turned back toward the road, the first blush of Christmas morning was stretching across the horizon and they could see light coming from Rick's house.

Rick opened the back door, blinking at their joined hands before grinning. "You're up early."

"You're one to talk," Darcy said.

Caroline laughed softly. "Is the coffee fresh?"

"Always."

They had barely stepped inside before the stampede hit and Sam, Walter, Lily, and Ellie ran at full speed into the kitchen in their festive Christmas pajamas that Rick had given them last night prior to bed.

"UNCLE DARCY! AUNT CAROLINE!"

"You're here, you're here, you're here! That means we can open presents now, right?!" Lily cried in excitement.

Rick grinned. "Seven o'clock, remember? It's only just six so breakfast first."

Lily's curls bounced as she pouted. "But we can't eat. We're too excited for food."

Caroline's amused glance met Darcy's and he couldn't help but shrug mischievously, "I mean, we did bring gifts early…"

"They're under the tree!" Lily squealed. "I promise I didn't peek but I *might* have sniffed one."

Caroline arched a brow. "You sniffed the presents?"

Walter rolled his eyes. "Only at least twice."

By seven, Marianne and Elinor arrived to round out the Christmas morning party with Marianne glowing as she beckoned to the young girl standing behind her. "Surprise!" she said, kissing Rick quickly. "This is my sister Maggie. She and Elinor are moving in with me!"

Lily shrieked, Maggie shrieked back, and Ellie clapped like she'd planned it all herself.

"Can we open presents now?" Sam begged as he looked up at the clock.

Dropping a handful of dirty silverware into the sink, Rick threw up his hands. "Okay, okay—*now* we can open presents."

Darcy crouched by the tree, playing Santa, and loved watching the expressions of joy and delight on everyone's faces as gifts were passed out and exclaimed over. Ellie squealed over her tricycle and the older kids exclaimed over their brand-new bicycles. Sam kissed his soccer ball. Walter clutched his fishing kit like it was pirate treasure. Marianne had even managed to shock Rick into silence when she'd given him tickets to a Prokofiev concert in San Diego. Then finally Lily opened her gift from Darcy and Caroline to reveal a pink collar, leash, and a photo of a golden retriever pup.

Her breath caught. "Is this… mine?"

Darcy's voice was thick. "Check the garage."

She bolted. Seconds later, her scream echoed throughout the house. "There's a puppy!"

The kids stampeded after her, returning with Lily proudly holding the sleepy golden retriever. Caroline's fingers laced with Darcy's as the room exploded in laughter and squeals and "Daniel the Brave" was declared the puppy's official name.

Rick waited until the chaos ebbed into cuddles and puppy kisses before clearing his throat. "All right, one more."

Four pairs of eyes swung toward him. He nodded to Marianne, who helped him pull a large, lumpy box out of the hall closet. It was wrapped in silver paper that crinkled with every eager tug as together the kids tore it open revealing a folded canvas tent printed with constellations, and accompanied by bundles of poles, and a small wooden sign that read *Adventurer's Hideout.*

For a moment there was silence as they took it in—then Walter whooped. Sam shouted, "It's a fort!" and Ellie squealed so loudly Daniel the puppy barked in alarm.

Within minutes, all four kids were on the floor, tugging pieces out, arguing over directions, and giggling as they tried to assemble the poles. The fort soon took shape in the corner, glowing with stars that could be seen when Rick's lantern was turned on inside the tent.

Ellie crawled in first, clutching her duck squad. "It's magic," she whispered.

Walter grabbed Marianne's kid sister Maggie's hand and tugged her along. "Come on! You're part of this too!" The two of them dove inside as Sam and Lily scrambled after them, their laughter bubbling out through the tent flap.

CHAPTER 27
Rick

Sam slammed his bedroom door so hard the hall picture frames rattled. Rick winced but didn't follow, not yet.

Downstairs, Ellie hummed as she brushed Daniel's puppy-soft ears, blissfully unaware of the storm upstairs. She didn't understand why Sam was angry, why Walter had suddenly packed a duffel, or how come sweet Lily had stomped outside with her chin lifted high like she was marching into battle.

Marianne stood in the kitchen doorway, worry threading her brow.

"You sure about this?" she asked.

"No," Rick admitted. "But Walter asked. And Lily… she's made up her mind."

"She's nine."

"She's Lily."

That earned him a reluctant smile.

Just as Marianne was poised to ask another question, Walter came trudging down the stairs with a stoic Darcy trailing behind with the car keys.

"Ready," Walter said, voice tight but steady.

Rick crouched to meet his eyes. "You sure about this, buddy? Last time hurt. Bad. You don't owe her anything."

Walter swallowed. "I know. But I need to know if she's changed. Even a little."

Marianne brushed his hair gently. "And if she hasn't?"

"Then I'll know for sure."

Sam appeared on the top step, glaring. "You're all idiots. She's not going to be different. She never is." His voice cracked. "Why are you even going, Daddy? She hurt you. She chained Lily. She doesn't deserve you."

"Sam—"

"I'm not going," he cut in, arms crossed. "And you shouldn't either."

The words stung because they weren't entirely wrong. But this wasn't about Louisa. It was about facing what she had done so they could finally choose their own paths forward.

"If she says something horrible again," Sam added, "don't come crying to me." Then he marched upstairs and slammed his door.

Rick breathed through the ache as Marianne squeezed his arm. "Call me when you leave the hospital," she said softly.

"I will."

The drive was thankfully quiet, the hum of tires filling the silence as the children avoided conversation if at all possible and Darcy seemed mindful of Rick's mood letting him pray and think in silence as he watched the road stretch leading him back up north toward a woman he never wanted to see again.

After a brief pit stop, Lily leaned against Rick's arm as she tugged nervously on her coat sleeve. "Do we have to go all the way?" she asked.

"We don't have to do anything, Sweetheart," he said gently. "But she is your mom, despite everything and—"

"She's not *my* mom," Lily fiercely interrupted.

"Then why are you even coming?" Walter growled as he turned away from the window for the first time all morning.

"Because she wanted to," Rick calmly reminded his son as he tried to reach out and reassure both kids but felt them both pull back into their internal worlds once more. Looking into the rear view mirror he saw Darcy's sympathetic smile and thanked God for such an amazing best friend who'd give up his entire day just to drive them to and from the mental hospital where Louisa had been sentenced for her crimes.

By they arrived at the hospital it was early afternoon and no one was in a good mood after sitting in the car so long that it was a quiet trio that waved to Darcy before walking inside and through security. The place smelled like antiseptic and regret and when Rick entered the visitation room for the first time he found it small and beige, the air too still, and swallowed down bile as he wanted to turn and run. If it weren't for the fact that both of his children were holding onto his hands so hard he thought they might break his fingers off, he probably would have ran right back to Darcy's car.

Some minutes later, Louisa entered the room looking smaller and hollower then he had ever seen her with her scrubs loose, hair limp, eyes shadowed. For one split second, Rick remembered the way she had looked when she had been drunk after her divorce from Tom Musgrove and had come tottering downstairs to thrust Sam into his arms. She might not be drunk this time but she looked unhinged and manic just like he remembered from seven years ago.

"I didn't think you'd actually come," she said to no one in particular as she took a seat before throwing a kiss at the muscular nurse who'd escorted her inside.

"It's Christmas," Rick answered flatly.

She looked at Lily without so much as a smile. "You've grown."

Lily sat up straighter. "Are you sorry for what you did to Daddy and me?"

Louisa blinked. "I don't expect you to forgive me, I just can't believe how big you've grown. You had been so shriveled up and puny when you had pneumonia in February. Funny enough, if I hadn't withheld medical help, your bastard of a father would probably never have wretched that phone away from me. That was my biggest mistake."

"You chained me up in a basement!" Lily exclaimed, in shock. "Your biggest regret is that you didn't give me medicine because then Dad wouldn't have taken your phone away?!"

Louisa flinched and, almost instinctively, reached for Lily's hand but Lily drew it back to her lap, shoulders tight and sure.

"I can't believe you are my mother," Walter finally spoke up as he stood and put his arm around Lily's trembling shoulders. "I don't hate you, Mom, but I don't love you either. Not anymore. Not after what you did to Daddy and all of us children."

There was nothing else to say.

179

"Come on," Rick murmured. "We've seen enough."

The kids fell asleep on the way home, leaning against each other in the back seat as they held hands. Rick sat in the front passenger seat, next to a quiet and sympathetic Darcy, staring unseeingly into the darkness ahead as Darcy drove them further and further away from Louisa. The ache in Rick's chest was heavier than he expected. Having heard Louisa he was convinced more than ever that she was gotten off lightly by being committed to a mental hospital instead of serving prison time.

Once he had gotten Lily and Walter into bed well past midnight, he stepped into Ellie's room and crouched beside her bed. "Hey, Little Love."

She blinked sleepily, smile tugging at her mouth as she dropped her thumb. Beyond the windows, the hush of the ocean was the only sound, and in that stillness time itself seemed to pause as he gazed at her innocent smile. "Daddy?"

"Yeah, I'm home." He brushed a curl off her forehead. "Go back to sleep."

Her little arms reached up, and he couldn't help but lift her into his arms as he sank onto the bed. She was so warm and soft and innocent and as he breathed in her baby powder scented sweetness he felt a sense of peace fill him up. Ellie's heartbeat against his chest, her little hand clutching at him like she trusted him with her whole world meant more than he could ever have expressed.

"You're safe," he whispered against her hair, his voice trembling. "You're safe, Little Love."

A whisper slipped from his lips without conscious thought as he cradled his baby against his chest, remembering the nights he'd rocked them both to sleep on his narrow cot in the basement.

"Praise You, God, for keeping Ellie safe." The words surprised him as if they had been waiting in the marrow of his bones.

Ellie stirred slightly and mumbled, "Daddy loves me."

His throat tightened. "Always."

Once daylight broke, life resumed in the Wentworth household as if nothing had happened the other day. Ellie could be found submerging Quackers in her bath before Rick could prevent the inevitable. The boys sprawled on their bedroom floor playing cards, while Daniel the puppy gnawing a piece of toast that had been dropped on the floor. Lily could be found reading one of her story books in the den. Despite how normal everything looked, Rick still carried that hollow ache from having seen Louisa again after so many months. He needed to talk to someone who understood what he was feeling so he texted Pastor Eddie.

"Come on over," Eddie replied, and fifteen minutes later Rick was knocking at the Ferrars' door after wrangling his next door neighbor George Knightley as a last minute babysitter.

"You look tired," Eddie said as he opened it.

"Exhausted and drained is more like it," Rick weakly laughed.

They made themselves comfortable in the living room with mugs of coffee as a faint gingerbread scent perfumed the room from a fresh batch of cookies Lucy had baked earlier that morning.

"Lucy's out," Eddie explained when Rick had asked. "With Tabitha and Caroline. Baby stuff."

"Baby stuff?"

He smiled, sheepish. "Yeah. She's eight weeks along."

"Wow. Congratulations."

"Thanks… I think."

Rick waited. Eddie leaned forward. "I should be excited. I am. But I can't deny that I am also terrified. We weren't even sure if we'd make it this far after her first couple miscarriages, and now… I'm going to be a dad. I don't even know what kind of husband I am, let alone what kind of father I'll be."

"Eddie, you don't have to have it all figured out," Rick said softly.

"Easy for you to say," he muttered.

"Trust me, it's not. I just drove over twelve hours in one day to see a woman who chained me and my kid up in a basement. She still wouldn't apologize. And I let my kids walk in there because I thought maybe it would give them closure." Rick swallowed. "And for them, it did. But for me… it just left questions. And this ache that won't quit."

"You did it because you love them," Eddie said quietly.

"I did it because I was afraid if I didn't, I'd be lying by pretending she didn't exist."

Eddie rubbed his face. "That's parenting. No clear roadmap. Some of us had good examples, some didn't. And some of us…" He exhaled. "…are still figuring out what it means to be men worth loving."

His voice trailed off, heavy with unspoken things, but Rick didn't push. They sat in silence, two men holding jagged edges together with duct tape and borrowed grace.

When Rick stood to leave, Eddie walked him to the door. "Just because someone fails you doesn't mean you failed, Rick. Okay?"

Rick nodded slowly. "Okay."

Back home, Ellie was napping upstairs while Sam was hiding behind a book on the couch as George coached Walter and Lily on the game of chess.

Rick stepped onto the back deck, leaning against the railing, staring at the dark curve of the ocean. His chest felt lighter, but there was still a hollow ache where Louisa's shadow used to be.

The sliding door whispered open behind him. He knew immediately whom it was before even turning around.

"You okay?" George gently asked.

"Yeah," he exhaled. "Better than I thought I'd be."

Rick shook his head slightly in thought. "Walter and Lily were so brave yesterday. Braver than I would have been."

George nodded as he leaned against the house. "You faced it. That matters. I lost my wife and our unborn son five years ago and I'm only now beginning to face it."

Rick nodded but kept his eyes on the waves. "There's something else I've been thinking about… my relationship with Marianne."

George's brow arched. "What about it?"

"She said once that she was worried about being with me because of Louisa… because of everything that woman took such as my virginity and… And I told her that Louisa didn't teach me how to want and care and love. I meant that but I don't know if she will ever fully believe that."

Rick's voice roughened. "Heck, sometimes I doubt people in this small-minded town even believe I was raped. The looks I get sometimes make me so mad."

George shifted against the siding, his limp noticeable even in the dim porch light. He exhaled hard, jaw tight. "Back when I was a detective, I saw it first-hand—men raped, boys too. Statistics and studies tell us that most men will never report it. The few who do report rape and sexual assault are laughed at, doubted, and even blamed. I believe you, Rick, for what it's worth."

Rick's chest clenched. He swallowed hard as he looked at the sunset.

George rubbed a hand over his jaw, his voice softer now. "I get the anger. When Emma was murdered, I didn't know what to do with the stares, the whispers. Everyone wanted me to 'move on,' and I couldn't. So I drank… a lot. I let grief and shame call the shots and it just about destroyed me."

His voice thickened, but steadied again. "But numbing it didn't heal me. Facing it has. Ironically, a lot of that determination is thanks to your boy, Walter. For all he's faced this year, he's shown more grit than most grown men I know. The trauma didn't break him and neither does it appear did his visit to see Louisa yesterday. It has made him wise beyond his years and his example made me realize I didn't have to stay broken either."

He shifted closer, leaning on the wall. "That's what you just did, Rick, just now. You faced up to your fears. And what you just said about Marianne's fears? About Louisa twisting love into something ugly? She needs to hear that from you."

184

For a long moment, the ocean's hiss filled the space between them. Rick finally dragged a hand through his hair, exhaling low.

George's gaze held him steady. "You've already walked through the fire. Don't be afraid to walk into love with that same honesty. Give Marianne the chance to know it from your lips. Trust her with it. She's earned that."

"You know," he said, tilting his head toward the street, "Marianne's not far from here. If you feel like she needs to hear this tonight, don't wait. We've got a couple hours before Darcy's bachelor shindig kicks off, so I can stick around with the kids while you run along."

Rick blinked at him, surprised. "You sure?"

A faint smile tugged at George's mouth, weary but steady. "I've spent too many years choking on words I should've said. Don't make that mistake, Rick. Don't let her wonder. If she's the one who makes you feel whole, don't wait to tell her."

Rick looked past him toward the ocean, heart hammering. Then he nodded, resolve settling into his chest. "Yeah. You're right." He glanced once more at the house, then back at George. "Thanks."

George gave a small shrug, the kind that said more than words. "Go. I've got this."

Rick exhaled and turned toward his car, each step carrying him closer to Marianne and to the truth he knew he couldn't hold back any longer.

When she opened the door, the porch light caught the glimmer of surprise in her eyes. "Rick? I was just getting ready for Caroline's bachelorette party. Are you all right?"

He swallowed hard, voice rough. "I had to see you. There's something I need to say, and I couldn't wait until morning."

Concern softened her features. "All right." She stepped aside, but he stayed rooted on the porch, the night air heavy with salt and silence.

His gaze held hers, steady now. "Yesterday, watching Lily stand up against Louisa at the hospital, it hit me again how wrong Louisa's warped version of love was. How it twisted everything good into something ugly. And you…" His voice thickened. "You're nothing like that. You're safe, and whole, and… honest in a way that can't even be compared to Louisa."

Marianne's eyes glistened, catching the porch light. "Rick…"

He brushed a strand of hair from her cheek. "I don't ever want you to doubt you're enough for me. Not after yesterday, not ever. Louisa didn't ruin me for love, Marianne. Rather, with her cruelty she made me grateful for the real thing, because now I know how rare it is when it's real."

Her breath caught as she lifted a hand to his jaw, thumb brushing his stubble. "You don't know how much I needed to hear that."

For a moment, neither moved. Then she stepped into him, forehead resting on his. "You're my safe place too, you know," she whispered. "Even when I'm scared I can't measure up to your past, you still make me feel like I belong right here."

Rick wrapped his arms around her and just held her, feeling the weight of the past drop another notch.

"I love you, Marianne," he said, voice low but certain.

Her eyes closed, tears slipping free as she whispered, "I love you too."

He kissed her softly, tenderly, as if sealing a promise of a man choosing a future no longer bound by fear.

"I used to wretch whenever Louisa kissed me," Rick admitted quietly. "Even after the rescue I couldn't imagine being kissed or kissing someone without needing to hurl my guts until our first kiss."

Her eyes softened, worry flickering. "Rick, we don't have to rush."

He shook his head, brushing her cheek with calloused fingers. "I don't mean that. What I'm trying—awkwardly, maybe—to say is that with you, I feel like myself again. With you, I'm able to experience love the way it was meant to be."

A breath hitched in her chest. "You mean that?"

He smiled faintly, almost in awe. "You make me feel free, Marianne. Like I get to choose what love looks like."

Her lips trembled, tears brightening her eyes. "And what does it look like?"

"This." He leaned in, kissing her again tenderly. It wasn't about proving anything or pretending to be healed. It was about choosing her, right here, right now.

When he pulled back, he brushed his thumb along her cheek, catching one of her tears, then tilted his head to press a kiss to her hand where it rested on his chest.

"Rick…" she whispered, "I've been so scared I wouldn't be enough for you. That you'd expect something I can't give yet."

He slid his hands to her shoulders, steady and sure. "You are enough. You're more than enough. I can't imagine my life without you. Being with you is healing and you even do wonders for the children."

A tear slipped free, and she smiled, relieved and radiant. "I'm so glad God brought us together, Rick Wentworth."

His hand brushed against the pocket where the ring box waited, and for a fleeting moment, he wondered if now was the time. If he should just drop to his knees and tell her everything his heart already knew.

But the thought passed. This moment belonged to healing, to honesty, to love spoken out loud. The proposal could wait. It would come soon enough and when it did, he wanted it to be perfect.

For now, it was enough to hold her close and thank God for bringing them this far.

CHAPTER 28

Darcy

Darcy stood on Rick's back deck, waves whispering beyond the fence. The winter air was cool and salted, laced with woodsmoke and the scent of pizza warming in the oven. String lights Rick and Eddie had rigged between the palms glowed warm and golden, turning the yard into a quiet haven.

Years ago, he'd have laughed at the idea of a bachelor party like this—no Vegas, no clubs, no flash. Back then, he thought joy had to be earned or bought. Now, watching Rick and Eddie bicker over firewood while George Knightley silently handed them the right tools, he felt something stronger than happiness. Gratitude.

Tabitha's husband Jordan lounged with a soda in his hand as Pastor Ned told a story about setting off a smoke alarm at youth camp. Meanwhile, Darcy's cousin William was being pulled into an animated debate with Walter and Sam about the merits of pineapple as a pizza topping, despite his initial unease.

Breaking into his thoughts, Rick nudged Darcy with a soda. "Not exactly wild, huh?"

"It's perfect," Darcy said, and meant it.

Rick studied him. "You look... lighter."

Darcy smiled faintly. "Because I am."

The sliding door opened and Caroline stepped out, cheeks pink from the cold, braids catching the light. Tabitha, Marianne, and Lucy followed with mugs of cocoa, their own night out at the karaoke bar clearly cut short.

"Hope we're not intruding," Caroline teased.

"You are," Rick deadpanned, "but nobody cares since you brought Marianne with you."

Marianne laughed, shaking her head. "You're impossible."

Caroline's loving gaze meanwhile locked onto Darcy. "You okay?"

"Better than okay."

Conversation flowed easily amongst the friends as the evening stars twinkled overhead. Darcy sat back, taking it all in. This was family—chosen, grace-built, and real. Caroline's fingers slipped into his under the edge of his chair. He glanced over and shared an intimate smile with the woman he was set to marry in just a couple days.

"You were thinking big thoughts," she whispered.

"About choices and about how they shape us."

"What did you choose?"

"You, of course," he grinned as he kissed her hand.

Her breath caught, fingers tightening in his grasp. "The future is ours," she whispered, leaning into him. "With you by my side, I can put to rest all of the judgments and prejudices that have been causing me bitterness lately. I know that in the end it is just you and me, Mr. Darcy."

"I am so lucky to have you, Caroline Bingley soon to be Darcy," he murmured.

"Good. Because I'm not going anywhere."

Behind them, Rick coughed.

"Lovebirds, cocoa's getting cold."

Caroline laughed but didn't let go of his hand.

Once the guests had left after wishing the soon to be married couple a good night, Darcy carried plates into the kitchen and found Caroline at the counter washing dishes, face softened by exhaustion and something tender.

"You ready?" he asked.

"Of course. Let me just grab my jacket."

After making their final farewells of thanks to Rick, they started to slowly walk along the water's edge, soaking in the moment, letting the hush of the waves etch it into memory.

"I'm so happy," Darcy said honestly. "In just a couple days, you're walking toward me, and I finally get to say I'm yours."

Her eyes shimmered. "And I get to say I'm yours."

Darcy's steps slowed until he stopped altogether, voice tightening with emotion.

"For years, I thought I had to be strong, flawless, above reproach. My pride made me measure myself—and others—by impossible standards. Aunt Catherine never let me forget what it meant to be a Darcy, and I carried those expectations like chains.

But you… you've taught me that love is patient, love is kind, love tells the truth without judgment. You've given me a glimpse of God's grace in a way I'd never fully received before."

Her breath caught, tears shining. "Oh, Darcy…"

Coming to a halt, his left hand slid to cradle the back of her neck, while his right hand brushed the line of her jaw as he kissed her softly at first, then deeper, weeks of restraint pooling into one slow, reverent kiss.

When he eased back, Caroline leaned her forehead against his. "I wouldn't care if your last name were Gardiner, or Hurst, or even Wickham," she teased. "The only name I care about carrying is yours."

Darcy huffed a laugh, shaking his head. "Wickham? What kind of name is that?"

She grinned. "Google it. I'm sure some poor soul out there actually has it."

Darcy chuckled, then brushed a kiss across her temple.

CHAPTER 29

Rick

The late afternoon sun stretched gold across the backyard, spilling across the waves beyond their fence. It was the day before New Year's Eve and Rick's family hadn't been down to the beach in days, not since prior to Christmas, so he packed sandwiches, fruit, and called the crew together for an impromptu picnic.

"Is Daniel coming?" Ellie tugged her pink duckie hat over her curls.

"Of course Daniel's coming," Rick said, clipping the puppy's leash. Daniel wriggled like he'd just been promised a steak buffet. "This is a family meeting. He's family."

Walter raised a brow as he slung the picnic blanket over his shoulder. "A family meeting? That sounds serious."

"It's not scary or bad," Rick promised. "It's more like a big, serious life decision moment."

"We can't move, Daddy!" Lily gasped as she tilted her head to look at Rick. "We're not going to leave Jane Austen Academy, are we?"

"Nope." He smiled, though his stomach felt the way it had before every deployment—tight, expectant. "We're not moving and you won't be changing schools anytime soon."

Lily noticeably relaxed at the clarification as she bent down to pet Daniel's fur.

"Are we getting another puppy?" Sam asked as he followed everyone outside of their backyard and onto the sandy beach.

"Don't push your luck," Rick laughed.

That earned him a chorus of groans and giggles.

As they made their way down the beach toward a picnic spot just before where the water touched the sand, Daniel bounded ahead carefree. Walter and Sam carried the cooler between them while Lily balanced the stack of plates and cups like precious cargo.

Minutes later, the blanket was spread, peanut butter and jelly sandwiches passed around, and everyone was settled waiting with bated breath for the big announcement.

Feeling all eyes on him, Rick waited until they'd prayed and each taken a bite before taking a deep breath.

"Okay. Family meeting time."

Walter frowned. "You're not sick, are you?"

"Nope."

"Quitting your job?" Lily asked.

"Nope again."

"Going on a date?" Sam asked through a mouthful of chips.

That made Rick laugh. "Closer. Actually… yeah, kind of like that. But it's a much bigger discussion I want to have with you kids."

They all froze, waiting. Even the dog sat up, ears perked like he understood something big was coming.

Rick took a breath. "How would you feel if I asked Miss Marianne to marry me?"

The silence lasted maybe four seconds.

Ellie squealed first, launching herself into his lap and nearly upending the plate of food. "We get Miss Marianne forever?!"

"That's the idea," he said, steadying her.

Lily's eyes went wide. "You mean she'd live with us?"

"Yup."

"And she'd be like… our mom?" Her voice wavered just slightly on the word.

Rick brushed a strand of hair from her face. "I know you never bonded with your mother, Sweetheart, but Louisa will always be your mother. Marianne does not want to overstep and won't require any of you to call her 'Mom' but she loves all of you. And I… I want her to be part of this family in a way that's permanent. How do you feel about that?"

Walter set down his sandwich slowly, his usual calm masking something more fragile. "She makes pancakes that don't burn half the time like yours do."

"Hey—" Rick started, but Walter grinned.

"And she sings when she thinks we're not listening," Lily added, smiling shyly.

Sam chewed on his peanut butter and jelly for a long second, like he wanted to argue, then shrugged. "Will she ban candy?"

"No bans allowed on candy," Rick promised.

Ellie hugged his neck so tight he could barely breathe. "I want her to be my mommy."

Something in his chest cracked and healed at the same time.

Walter cleared his throat. "She makes you happy," he said simply. "You didn't laugh much before her."

"She does make me happy," Rick admitted, voice thick. "Happier than I ever thought I could be."

"Then I'm good with it."

"Me too," Lily chimed in.

"Me three!" Ellie squeaked.

Sam pointed a chip at him. "Okay, but what were you going to do with the ring if we had said no?"

Rick chuckled, patting the ring box in his pocket. "Probably cry, return it, and live alone in a cave with only Daniel."

Ellie gasped. "You can't take Daniel away!"

"That's why I'm glad you said yes," Rick said, kissing the top of her head. "Now we can all live together happily ever after like in your storybooks, Little Love."

They finished lunch and decided to walk along the tide line. Ellie soon was chasing Daniel while Walter and Lily argued good-naturedly about whether "Captain Barkington" was an acceptable nickname for the dog.

Rick hung back a few paces, watching them. His beautiful children had been through too much, they had seen things no kids should, yet still they carried this wild, stubborn joy that could not be extinguished. He thought about Marianne's soft smile when she read bedtime stories, her patience when he panicked in the middle of crowds, and the way she hugged Ellie like she'd been born into her arms. Together they would be as perfect a family as possible, he imagined.

"Hey, Dad!" Walter called. "You coming?"

Rick jogged to catch up, slipping an arm around both of his sons' shoulders. "Yeah, Bud. I'm coming."

Ellie shrieked with laughter as Daniel tugged her toward the waves, Lily trying to help while Sam pretended to referee. Their voices carried across the sand, bright and alive, and Rick ran the last few steps, grabbing Ellie and spinning her in a circle until they both fell laughing into the sand.

Rick wasn't just surviving. He was running headlong into the future and he couldn't wait to meet it.

CHAPTER 30

Darcy

The beach house smelled like cinnamon and fried plantains, with a faint undertone of glue from the DIY centerpiece station underway at the dining table.

Rick was outside in the backyard with Eddie and Jordan, stringing lights between the palms for tomorrow's ceremony. Indoors, Caroline and Tabitha moved in rhythm at the kitchen island, passing utensils back and forth like they'd been cooking together for years. Marianne and Elinor glazed salmon and tossed a citrus-avocado salad, humming along with the wedding playlist Caroline had put together.

Darcy lingered in the doorway longer than necessary, drawn to Caroline and the beautiful vision of her in her bridal glow. She looked radiant as she laughed at something someone said. She looked like she belonged here.

The doorbell rang just as Rick returned with extra command hooks. A pinch of unease crawled up his spine. Life rarely stayed perfect for long in Croft Beach, and he knew instinctively the door wouldn't bring good news.

Unaware of the tension Darcy was experiencing, little Ellie shot up from her coloring spot. "I'll get it!"

"No running!" Marianne called out from the kitchen.

Ellie sprinted anyway, flinging the door open just as Darcy and Rick reached the entryway.

And there they were. His little sister, Georgie, smiling too brightly. And next to her was the one woman he'd hoped not to have to see again. Lizzie looked decidedly uncomfortable holding a wrapped gift in her hands.

"Surprise," Georgie said, almost sheepish.

Darcy's jaw tightened. "What are you doing here?"

"We were in town," Georgie said, "and I thought… we thought… we just wanted to drop off a wedding gift."

Lizzie's posture was hesitant, her voice softer than he remembered. "We didn't mean to intrude. I just wanted to wish you well."

From behind him, Caroline's voice came steady and even. "You already did, Lizzie. At Christmas."

Lizzie nodded, her gray gaze flicking to Caroline and away again. "Yeah. I guess I did."

Ellie's small voice piped up, uncertain. "Daddy says surprises are only fun when everyone's happy."

Rick who had been standing silently beside Darcy during this exchange finally spoke up. "Darcy?"

"I've got it," Darcy said, then looked at Georgie and Lizzie. "Thank you for the gift. We'll open it later." He accepted the package and stepped aside, not inviting them in.

Lizzie hesitated, then gave Caroline a tentative smile. "I meant what I said that night. I hope Croft Beach treats you better."

Caroline held her gaze. "So do I."

Something like relief crossed Lizzie's face before she stepped back. "Congratulations, Darcy and Caroline."

"Thank you," Caroline said quietly.

Georgie murmured her own goodbye, and then they were gone, leaving Darcy holding the wedding gift in his arms.

Rick closed the door and locked it with a quiet finality that felt like sealing off more than just a draft. The silence that followed was cleansing, like a storm finally rolling out to sea.

Marianne peeked in, eyebrows arched. "Do I even want to know?"

Rick sighed as he shook his head at Marianne before turning back to Darcy and Caroline. "Do I need to hide the sharp objects?"

Caroline blinked fast, steadying herself. "I'm okay."

Darcy set down the gift on the table so that he could brush a bit of flour from her cheek with his thumb. "You're more than okay."

She leaned her forehead against his for a moment, her breath shaky but evening out as she smiled.

From the kitchen, Eddie shouted, "Lucy called and says she's on the way with the flowers!"

Rick clapped his hands. "All right, folks. Decorations don't hang themselves."

Just like that, the rhythm returned. Footsteps, laughter, music flowed back into place like a tide reclaiming the shore.

Sometime later, on Caroline's porch the soon-to-be married couple stood at the door, arms wrapped around each other as they looked out at Croft Beach's sleepy main street.

Darcy sighed as he inhaled the scent of her shampoo. "I love you, Mrs. Darcy."

She couldn't help but laugh as she pulled back to look up in his face. "Hey. I'm not Mrs. Darcy until tomorrow so you better be there on time."

Darcy laughed in turn and kissed her warmly, pressing his hard mouth against her eager lips as if he couldn't get enough of her sweetness.

They stood there for a moment in a quiet that wasn't heavy, just rich with everything they'd endured to reach this day and full of the promises of tomorrow.

"I can't believe we're doing this," he murmured.

Her lips curved faintly. "I can."

When she finally turned, her eyes were soft but steady. "I spent so much of my life waiting for someone to see me and not try to change me. At first you…"

He flinched because there were so many episodes of their past that weren't pretty and where he didn't come out as anything resembling a prince charming.

"And then you didn't," she added quickly. "You let me speak for myself. You didn't try to save me nor apologize for me. You let me take up space, even when it was messy."

He threaded his fingers through hers, his voice low. "You never have to be small again, Caroline. Not with me."

"There's still prejudice out there," she said. "Croft Beach won't magically wake up changed. But I'm not leaving. I'd rather we face it here—where I've found my voice— together, than run just to feel safe."

Pride surged through him, fierce and unshakable. "My instinct is to want to protect you," he admitted. "But I know now that's not always what you need."

Her eyes softened. "No. Sometimes protection feels like control. Like being told to sit back, be quiet, and stay safe." Her voice firmed, beautiful and certain. "But I don't want to be safe if it means being silent."

He cupped her cheek. "You'll never have to be silent again. Not with me."

Her eyes shimmered. "Thank you for seeing me. All of me."

"I love you," he whispered. "Even the messy parts."

A laugh slipped out, quiet and breathless, before she wrapped her arms around his waist. He held her close, kissed her temple, and felt the old fear fall away.

"I was so afraid I'd lose you," he murmured.

"Thank you for fighting for me, for fighting for us," she said softly. "Not like some romantic hero. You fought by listening, by changing, and most of all by showing up."

He smiled faintly. "No one puts Baby in a corner."

"You did not just quote *Dirty Dancing* at me," she whispered, laughing into his chest.

"I had to watch it on repeat when Georgie was obsessed with Patrick Swayze. It left an impression."

Her laughter faded, replaced by something warmer, heavier. She lifted her face, and he couldn't resist the opportunity to kiss her one more time.

"Caroline…" he breathed, pulling back to kiss her forehead tenderly. His voice was ragged. "If I don't stop now—"

Her smile curved slow and knowing. "Then stop," she whispered, though her fingers still curled into his shirt. "Because tomorrow, you're mine. All mine, Mr. Darcy."

That promise steadied him. He kissed her once more slow, deep, reverent before stepping back reluctantly. "You're worth every second of waiting."

Her grin was bold and sure. "Good. Because I'm not going anywhere."

The tide whispered beyond them, steady and sure, as if creation itself was bearing witness to tomorrow's vows.

CHAPTER 31
Rick

The scent of maple syrup and vanilla filled the kitchen before the first waffle even hit the iron. Rick had added a splash of vanilla to the batter at Ellie's prompting and now she sat at the table with Quackers in one hand and a fork in the other, ready like breakfast was the main event of the day.

Walter stood beside him, cracking eggs into a bowl with surgical precision, brows furrowed like he was disarming a bomb. Sam circled the kitchen like a boxer in training, throwing jabs at imaginary opponents and making sizzling sound effects to match the bacon popping on the stove.

And Lily, Rick's steady right hand, was on his other side arranging berries and banana slices like a finalist on a cooking show, lips pursed in concentration.

"Dad, can I flip the next one?" Sam asked, peeking over the edge of the waffle iron.

"Not yet," Rick said with a grin. "It has to be sunshine golden first."

Walter smirked. "That's not a real color."

"It is in this house."

The kids laughed. Ellie dropped Quackers onto the table and declared, "Quackers wants chocolate chips in his!"

"He can wait his turn," Rick said, leaning down to bump his nose gently against hers in a playful Eskimo kiss before sliding past with the spatula. Ellie squealed, clutching Quackers back to her heart like she'd just won something priceless.

Sunlight streamed through the window, glinting off the backyard fence and the shiny new bikes leaning near it still a little dusty from their maiden rides the other day.

The morning already hinted at what an amazing new year lay ahead.

No chains.

No darkness.

No Louisa.

Last New Year's Eve, he hadn't even known the date. He'd stopped counting days altogether and had to rely on Louisa to tell him what date it was never knowing if she was telling the truth or lying to amuse herself. The cellar had been so bitterly cold it sank into his bones, leading to Lily's terrible spell of pneumonia in the new year when he thought he might lose his firstborn.

Louisa had laughed when he cried and punished him when he prayed. Nevertheless, somehow, God had heard him anyway.

Because now his life consisted of all this.

Laughter.

Waffles.

Sunlight.

His kids were in pajamas, bedhead wild, arguing over syrup and spoon privileges like it was life or death. Rick didn't take a second of it for granted.

"Lily," he said, "grab me the cinnamon?"

She passed it over, leaning against the counter. "Is it weird you're not getting married today?"

He glanced at her, startled. "You think I should be?"

She shrugged. "You will. I can tell. Ellie keeps saying *when*, not *if*."

His chest gave a quiet flip. "*When* feels like the right word."

She nodded and went back to arranging fruit in rainbow order. She didn't need him to say anything more.

The timer finally dinged. He opened the waffle iron, steam curling out like some kind of benediction.

"Sunshine golden," he declared, sliding it onto a plate.

"Score!" Sam whooped.

The children dove into breakfast with syrup-drizzled enthusiasm as Rick glanced at the clock and froze.

"Kids, hustle up," he said, starting to unplug the waffle iron. "Uncle Darcy's going to be here in thirty minutes, and we need this place to look picture-perfect for his wedding."

Ellie gasped. "We have to look fancy!"

Walter groaned. "Does fancy mean ties?"

206

"Yes."

"Can Daniel wear a tie too?" Ellie asked, already tugging on the puppy's collar.

"We'll talk about it after breakfast."

As the children finished inhaling their pancakes and stacked the dishes in the dishwasher before racing to the bathrooms, Rick took a chance to enjoy the peace and quiet and sat down, picking up the fountain pen the kids had given him for Christmas, Darcy's idea, he was sure, and opened his journal to a clean page:

December 31

I used to think healing would look like silence. Like sleep. Like forgetting. But it doesn't.

Healing looks like this kitchen.
It looks like syrup stuck in Ellie's curls and a half-burnt waffle I eat anyway because Sam grins when I do.
It sounds like Walter's laugh echoing off the walls, Lily humming carols under her breath, and Ellie tugging on my sleeve to ask if we can go to the beach after Uncle Darcy marries Aunt Caroline.

Healing isn't quiet.
It's noise.
It's chaos.
It's life.

And it's grace.

Thank You, God, for showing up when I least believed You would.
For proving that survival isn't the end of the story.
You've given me more. You've given me resurrection.

From panic attacks in crowded stores…
to peace at this messy table.
From chains that mocked me…
to children who trust me.
From silence that once felt like death…
to laughter that tastes like life.

Today is full of promise.
My kids.
My home.
My God.

Thank You.

He closed the journal, heart steady, and stood. "Okay," he said, clapping his hands. "Fancy clothes, kids! I better see you all in your wedding finery when I walk down the hall. We've got a wedding to get ready for."

He smiled, tucking the journal under his arm. This was life. Loud, sweet, unbroken and steady as the tide. He wasn't about to miss a second of it.

CHAPTER 32

Darcy

Darcy arrived at Rick's cottage with nerves burned off, replaced by something steadier—excitement, hope, clarity. He tugged lightly at the lapel of his custom suit. It was a tradition his father had started for his own wedding and one he was proud to carry on. The charcoal wool Caroline had chosen was soft and perfectly tailored, hand-stitched not for vanity but for permanence and for moments meant to last. Today was one of those moments.

It was finally happening.

The front yard had been transformed into something simple yet perfect: string lights draped between palms, white folding chairs fanning toward a small canopy borrowed from the Jane Austen Academy's supply shed. Rick stood at the aisle's edge with George, Eddie, and Ned, jackets off and sleeves rolled up like they'd been working until the last possible minute.

"About time," Rick said, pulling Darcy into a quick hug. "You ready?"

"I've never been more ready," Darcy answered, voice low but certain.

"Then let's get you married." Rick grinned, moving to his place as best man.

Inside, the kids were dressed and buzzing with energy, darting around eager to catch the grand moment they'd all been awaiting. Rick's girls glowed in pale gold dresses with ribbon sashes, Walter stood proud in his little vest, and Sam, of course, had paired superhero socks with his dress shoes.

A soft piano melody cued the men that the moment was finally here. With a sigh of elation, Darcy turned instinctively toward the stairs.

Ellie came first, tiny bouquet in hand, her sparkly gold dress twirling around her legs. Her curls bounced with each careful step.

And then Caroline appeared and everything stopped.

She wore an ivory gown that fit like poetry—modern and elegant. It hugged her figure, then softened into a flowing skirt that caught the light. Her braids were swept into a low bun, a few strands loose to frame her face, and a golden gele-inspired comb nestled in the back as a quiet, loving nod to her late mother. She didn't carry flowers, just her father's well-worn Bible, pressed to her heart.

Darcy's chest tightened, breath catching painfully in his throat. She was luminous and she was his.

Caroline and Ellie were halfway down the stairs when the front door eased open. A nervous Georgie slipped in, shoulders hunched as if bracing to be thrown out. Darcy crossed quickly, hugged his little sister tightly to himself. She stiffened, likely braced for rejection, but then clung to him for a brief, desperate beat too.

"I didn't want to miss it," she whispered.

"I'm glad you came," he murmured, guiding her to a seat beside Elinor and Tabitha.

When Caroline and Ellie reached the makeshift aisle's end, Ellie lifted her chin proudly. "I give you away now, Aunt Caroline."

A ripple of laughter moved through the room. Lucy, standing in her place of honor as matron of honor, discreetly dabbed at her eyes.

Ned stepped forward, Bible in hand, voice warm and sure. "Welcome, family and friends. We are gathered here not in a cathedral or grand hall, but in a home—a place of belonging, laughter, and grace. I can think of no better place to mark this joyous union."

He looked at Darcy. "I've known you since you were a boy in shoes scuffed and at odds with your Sunday best. I watched you wrestle with pride, grow into humility, and choose love over control. You're not the boy I once knew. You have become a man who serves, who listens, and who loves well."

Then to Caroline: "When I first met you, you were searching—curious and bold, unwilling to settle for easy answers. You found faith not because someone told you to, but because truth stirred your soul. You have let God shape you. It hasn't been an easy road, but you fought for godliness and love. Caroline, you are a woman of strength and grace, and it's been my honor to walk part of this journey with you."

Caroline's eyes glistened, but she smiled, shoulders squaring.

Ned gestured toward the candles on the mantle. "We honor those who are not with us in body but surely present in spirit. Darcy's parents, George and Anne Darcy, and Caroline's parents, William and Nche Bingley, are sorely missed by their children but we bless their loving example today. May their memory be a blessing for you both, Darcy and Caroline."

A quiet reverence settled over the room as Ned smiled. "And now, the vows."

Darcy reached for Caroline's hands, steadying her trembling fingers in his. "In college, I never imagined myself here," he said, voice thick. "But God gave us a second chance. You challenged me, saw me, and refused to let me settle for fear or control. You made me laugh. You taught me joy. You made me a better man. Caroline Bingley, I vow to love you, to honor you, to stand by you, and to grow with you, as your faithful companion, all the days of our lives—even imperfectly."

Caroline's hands trembled, but her smile was warm, threaded with humor. "After years of chasing you—" she paused as laughter rippled through the room, "—I thought I was fine on my own. But grace is wild like that because it gives what we don't deserve. And you were worth waiting for. Fitz Darcy, I promise to love you boldly, to walk beside you, and to see you always through the eyes of grace."

A tear slid down Darcy's cheek but he didn't care.

"By the power vested in me as a minister of the Gospel and as a witness to your love," Ned said softly, "I now pronounce you husband and wife. You may kiss the bride."

Darcy didn't hesitate. He slid one arm firmly around Caroline's waist and the other to the small of her back, drawing her close as he kissed her like the rest of the world had fallen away. It wasn't rushed—it was slow, deep, reverent, full of every unspoken promise he'd ever carried for her. She melted against him, arms curling around his shoulders, lips parting in quiet surrender.

Somewhere behind them, Rick muttered, "Shield the kids!" and laughter rippled through the room, but Darcy didn't stop, not until Caroline smiled against his mouth and whispered breathlessly, "Hi, husband."

He kissed her again, harder this time, needing one more taste, one more second to be sure this was real.

"Hi, Mrs. Darcy."

When they finally parted, Ellie clapped wildly. "Yay!"

Darcy glanced toward the back of the room and caught Georgie standing, tears streaking her cheeks, hands clasped like she was holding something fragile. Their eyes met, and for the first time in weeks there was no anger, no wall between brother and sister, only understanding. She mouthed, *She's perfect for you.* He grinned as he nodded back.

"May I have the honor of presenting for the first time ever, Mr. and Mrs. Darcy."

Ned grinned as the room erupted in cheers. Rick laughed as all of his children barreled forward to hug Darcy and Caroline, as Lucy, Marianne, and Tabitha wiped happy tears from their eyes.

Caroline met Darcy's gaze, mischief dancing in her smile. "You're mine now, Mr. Darcy."

Darcy kissed her one final time, fierce and sure, savoring the warmth of her lips and the shiver that ran through him before he whispered against her mouth, "Always."

Caroline's eyes glistened as she smiled, bold and certain. "Then let's begin forever, starting now."

CHAPTER 33

Rick

Rick had never felt more love in a single place. Less than a year after being rescued from Louisa's cellar, he was standing behind the long folding table moonlighting as a reception bar. He had one arm around Marianne's shoulders while the other held a glass of apple cider as his friends and children watched and waited.

The newlyweds, Darcy and Caroline, sat near the outdoor fireplace hands linked, foreheads touching now and then. Lantern light caught the gold pins in Caroline's hair. Darcy's tie was already loosened. They looked happy and like they were in their own private paradise.

Finally he could put it off no longer and tapped his glass to get the bride and groom's attention.

"I've known this guy"—Rick jerked his chin toward Darcy—"since we were five years old at Jane Austen's Academy and he decided to give me a wedgie by hanging me from the coat hook. I watched him get things right and get things wrong more often than not. I saw him fail time and time again and yet keep showing up anyway. I watched Darcy risk his reputation to stand with me when I had nothing and no one after Marianne rescued Lily and me from the cellar. Then I watched him fall in love with a woman who doesn't care about pride."

With a smile at Darcy, Rick turned to the woman sitting beside him and took a deep breath. "Caroline, I was flabbergasted when Marianne told me that you and Darcy were a couple. Back in college, you were the last person I imagined ending up here. But God's grace has written a different story, and you've proven me wrong more times than I can count since the moment you slipped the anklet on my daughter's scarred ankle. You have proven what a difference God has made in your life. You opened your heart not only to my kids, to me, and somehow to this whole town no matter how many times they turned their back on you. Tonight feels bigger, warmer, because of you."

Caroline's eyes filled, and Darcy squeezed her hand.

"I'm a dad who spent last New Year's Eve chained to a wall," Rick continued quietly. "Tonight I get to feed my kids cake and watch my best friend kiss his bride. That's God. That's grace. And the two of you—" he pointed at them with his glass "—are a neon sign that says He's not done redeeming things and yes, as Darcy once told me, His plans are better."

"To Darcy and Caroline," he finished, lifting his glass.

"To Darcy and Caroline!" the room echoed.

They drank cheerfully as Rick sat back down next to Marianne, finally exhaling. His duties as best man were finally over. Marianne leaned into him, cheek warm against his arm. "That was perfect," she whispered.

He was just starting to breathe again when Lily stood up. She tugged Walter, who grabbed Sam, who dragged Ellie. The four of them marched to the center of the patio and turned to face him like a kid-sized firing squad. Lily held something behind her back.

"Can we do our presentation now?" she asked Darcy, earnest as sunrise.

Darcy grinned. "Definitely."

They flipped a poster open:
MARRY US MISS MARIANNE
—in full crayon glory, stick figures, glitter glue, and one very excited duck doodle.

Marianne's eyes widened, hand flying to her mouth.

Walter stepped forward like a lawyer presenting evidence. "He already bought the ring."

Sam nodded. "He got it at the jewelry store."

Ellie jumped up and down. "It was soooo pretty!"

"It's in his pocket," Walter added.

Lily crossed her arms. "So, what are you waiting for?"

Rick stood slowly, feeling a dozen sets of eyes on him. His heart pounded in amazement that this was really happening.

Darcy appeared at his side like a smug fairy godfather and clapped a firm hand on his back. "Well, Wentworth? You've had the ring long enough."

Rick looked back at Marianne. Her eyes shimmered with surprise and a hope he could not ignore. She looked like she might either burst into laughter or tears, or possibly both, but most of all she looked like she couldn't wait a second more before he got down on his knees and put the ring on her finger.

"I… I didn't plan this," he admitted. "I had something planned for tomorrow." He exhaled, voice shaking. "But maybe this is better. Because it's real. It's us."

He reached into his suit jacket and pulled out the small ring box, and his journal. Setting the ring box on a table, he flipped open his journal to a page where his handwriting slanted messy and uneven.

They'll say she's too much—too loud, too soft,
Too bold, too different, too far off
From what the world expects of love.
Not thin enough, not white enough,
Not tame enough, not young enough.

They'll whisper questions with narrowed eyes,
Judge by shade, or shape, or size—
But they don't see what I have seen:
The strength she holds behind the sheen,

The faith that roots her soul so deep,
The love she gives—wide, wild, and deep.
She lifts my children when they fall,
She listens when I can't speak at all.

She doesn't fit a perfect frame—
And God, I thank Him just the same.
So let the world weigh what it will—
With every fear, and stare, and chill.

Their prejudice has no domain
Where Christ is King and love remains.
If she'll have me, come what may,
I'll choose her every single day.

With a nervous smile, Rick got down on his knee and held the ring up to Marianne. "Marianne Dashwood, would you do me and my children the greatest honor and choose to make a life with us? We're not the perfect package deal, but if you choose us, you will always be loved and cared for."

Silence fell for a beat.

Then Ellie shouted, "Say yes!"

Marianne stepped forward, eyes brimming, and knelt with him. "Yes," she whispered—soft, certain, everything he had prayed for.

The party erupted. Out of Rick's peripheral view he could see that even Marianne's older sister Elinor was clapping, smiling with joy.

Grinning at how God had brought all of them together, Rick looked at his beautiful fiancée and kissed her. It was not careful or polite, but a claiming kiss, one that healed and promised and said he was finally home.

"You have no idea how long I've waited to kiss you like that," he whispered when they finally broke apart.

Marianne smiled, flushed and radiant. "Then do it again."

So he did. Slower. Deeper. Reverent. Her fingers curled into the front of his suit jacket, pulling him closer, deepening the kiss until cheers blurred into nothing and all he could focus on was her soft lips against his and the warm press of her body.

It wasn't careful. It wasn't polite. It was reverent. It was a promise—a claiming—that said *you're safe, you're mine, and I'm never letting go*.

She smiled against his lips, breathless, whispering just for him, "Again."

So he kissed her again, savoring every second, because after everything they'd survived, this love deserved to burn bright and unapologetic like fire catching in the night. And he didn't care who saw.

EPILOGUE – EDDIE FERRARS

The house shimmered with warmth—string lights glowing like stars, soft music in the background, and children's laughter echoing down the hallway. Inside, Darcy and Caroline's wedding reception was winding down into the kind of quiet joy that made a house feel like home.

Eddie Ferrars, however, stood alone in the backyard, staring at the restless waves. The salt air cut colder than he expected.

Lucy had gone home two hours ago, worn out from pregnancy sickness. He should have gone with her. He should have been at home rubbing her back, giving her spoonfuls of ice chips, whispering comfort, and holding her hair the way he promised *the day they said I do.*

Instead, he stayed. She had insisted he stay, but deep down he knew that she had hoped he'd argue and go home with her.

Just as he was about to head back in to make his farewells, the door creaked behind him.

He didn't need to turn. He already knew who it was that had come outside.

"Elinor," he said quietly, taking in her appearance.

She stepped beside him, jacket pulled tight against the coolness of the night, raven hair escaping her updo to caress her pale neck. He frowned when he saw that her eyes were too bright, too glassy. A half-finished champagne flute dangled in her hand.

Elinor's gaze flicked toward the window where laughter spilled from every corner of the house—couples linked together, kids tangled in blankets, friends shoulder to shoulder. Eddie could imagine what she was thinking and felt sympathy for her. Everyone was paired up. All felt the sense of belonging. Except her.

"Remember New Year's Eve, sophomore year?" she asked softly.

His lips twitched. "When I lit my coat on fire trying to impress you?"

Her laugh was soft, familiar. Dangerous. "You always had the worst timing."

"I still do," he admitted.

A silence stretched between them, fragile and wrong.

"Do you ever wonder…" Her voice thinned almost to nothing. "What might've happened, Eddie? If we hadn't made the choices we did?"

He swallowed hard. "Elinor—"

She stepped closer. Too close.

"I'm not try… trying to make a mess of any… anything," she slurred, eyes shimmering with something aching and reckless. "I just needed to know if I was ever… more than a what-if."

Before he could process it, she kissed him.

Soft. Slow. A heartbeat too long.

Eddie jerked back as if scalded. "Elinor—"

That's when he saw them.

Caroline.
Marianne.

The two women stood frozen in the doorway.

Marianne's eyes widened in disbelief.
Caroline's jaw tightened, her heartbreak unmistakable.

And then—

"TEN!"

The countdown thundered from inside the house, oblivious to the scene on the deck.

"NINE!"

Elinor staggered back, horror dawning on her flushed face. "I—I'm sorry—I just—"

"EIGHT!"

Eddie turned toward the door, panic slamming into his chest.

"SEVEN!"

Lucy's voice rang from the hallway, warm and trusting: "Eddie? I couldn't let you ring in the new year alone!"

"SIX!"

The kids were laughing near the kitchen, Ellie's voice rising: "Come quick, it's almost time!"

"FIVE!"

His hands shook. The scent of Elinor's perfume clung to his jacket like a curse.

"FOUR!"

He couldn't breathe. Couldn't move.

"THREE!"

He had kissed Elinor.
Caroline saw.
Marianne saw.
And Lucy… Lucy was inside.

"TWO!"

His chest ached, sick with shame, his pulse thundering in his ears.

"ONE!"

Cheers erupted, fireworks splitting the night sky in gold and silver as Lucy stepped through the back door heading his way with a big smile of love and trust.

But Eddie Ferrars stood frozen, staring at the woman he loved all the while feeling the weight of the mistake he had just made. A single thought pounding through him like a siren:

What have I done?

* * *

To be continued in Book Four: The Cost of Betrayal

THE COST OF BETRAYAL

(Jane Austen's Men, Book 4)

One impulsive kiss shatters Pastor Edward Ferrars's marriage and sends him spiraling into guilt and grief.

When Lucy suffers a heartbreaking loss, Eddie begs for forgiveness but she is too wounded to trust again. Desperate for change, he and Lucy are persuaded to join Rick, Darcy, and Ned Bertram and their wives on a journey abroad, where he must learn that winning Lucy's heart will require far more than apologies.

Through Eddie's struggle and Rick Wentworth's heartfelt reflections, *The Cost of Sensibility* reveals that sensibility costs everything, but God's plan leads to joy.

PREORDER ON AMAZON.COM

DID YOU LIKE THIS BOOK?

If *The Weight of Prejudice* inspired you, encouraged you, or simply kept you turning pages late into the night—would you consider leaving a review?

Your words matter more than you know. Reviews help other readers discover new stories and give indie authors like me the chance to keep writing, sharing, and growing.

Whether it's one sentence or a thoughtful reflection, your voice makes a difference.

✒ **Leave a review on Amazon, Goodreads, or wherever you buy your books.**

Thank you for reading. Thank you for feeling. Thank you for sharing this journey with Darcy, Caroline, Rick, and Marianne.

With gratitude,
Joy Michelle Austin

ACKNOWLEDGEMENTS

Writing *The Weight of Prejudice* proved even harder than writing *Half Agony, Half Hope* which was something I didn't think was possible. Stepping into the shoes of Jane Austen's most beloved hero, Darcy, carried enormous expectations. Pairing that with themes as deeply personal and complex as racism, prejudice, and the pain of being misunderstood made this one of the most emotionally demanding journeys I've ever taken as a writer.

To the readers of *Half Agony, Half Hope*, thank you for embracing Rick's story with compassion, for cheering him on, and for reminding me why stories of redemption, justice, and healing matter. Your encouragement gave me the courage to keep writing.

To my dear friends: Ashli, Brynn, Ginger, Laura, Laurie, Maegan, Misty, Pam, Tabitha, and so many others, thank you for your prayers, laughter, voice memos, and unshakable support. You carried me through the hardest chapters and celebrated every breakthrough with joy. I'm so grateful to have you in my corner.

A special thanks to the Women at the Inkwell at South Shores Church in Dana Point, California. Your faithfulness and prayers meant the world to me. Thank you for believing not just in this book, but in the healing power of storytelling itself.

And finally, to every reader who has experienced prejudice firsthand—whether through the color of your skin, the shape of your body, your cultural heritage, or the way you love—this story is for you. May you find hope, belonging, and the reminder that you are deeply and unconditionally loved.

To the One who makes all things new—may every page reflect Your truth, Your grace, and Your relentless love.

ABOUT THE AUTHOR

Joy Michelle Austin is a novelist, blogger, and storyteller whose love for literature led her to earn an English degree in creative writing. A lifelong admirer of Jane Austen, she blends classic themes with contemporary issues in her *Jane Austen's Men* series—gritty, emotionally charged stories of faith, redemption, and romance.

Her latest novel, **The Weight of Prejudice**, follows the beloved Darcy as he confronts the deeply personal realities of racism, pride, and public expectation in a modern world. A sequel to her acclaimed debut, **Half Agony, Half Hope**, this book continues Joy's exploration of emotionally complex men learning to love, forgive, and rebuild.

Beyond fiction, Joy is the voice behind **The Joyous Living**, a blog where she shares thoughtful reviews and insights on film, literature, travel, and the performing arts. Her collaborations include trusted brands such as Disney, Affirm Films, Amazon, Segerstrom Center for the Arts, bestselling author Tracie Peterson, and more.

Whether through novels or blog posts, Joy is passionate about telling stories that speak to the soul—stories rooted in hope, healing, and the beauty of second chances.

Connect with Joy:
www.thejoyousliving.com

BOOKS BY JOY MICHELLE AUSTIN